Hunter / Prey

Tony McFadden

Beach Nut Press

Copyright © 2017 Tony McFadden

Re-issue 2024

ISBN: 978-0-6456733-9-5

DEDICATION

For All The Nasty Women

ACKNOWLEDGMENTS

You're reading this due to the support of many beta-readers who have helped enormously. Thanks also to the Northern Beaches Writers' Group, again, for their collective input to the opening chapters.

You're an awesome group of writers.

.

Chapter One

Mac Durridge stepped out of the limousine in front of the Avoca Beach Theatre and looked at the crowd lining the red carpet. He tugged at the sleeves of the impossibly starched shirt, aligning the shirt cuffs with the tuxedo cuffs. He felt as uncomfortable as he looked.

Steve Ryan, star of the movie, stepped out next and turned to help Jessie. She was tall, lithe and tanned, even in the middle of winter. Her blonde hair was tied up in a loose, messy bun. Mac looked at her and smiled. She was beaming, a far distance from the mess she'd been in when Steve first came into their lives six months earlier.

The crowd erupted at Steve's arrival and the continuous sound of camera shutters was almost deafening. Mac leaned into Steve's ear. "This turns you on, doesn't it?"

"Hey, there's ladies present." Steve smiled, impossible white teeth in his deeply tanned face, topped with perfectly highlighted hair. Accented by a recently healed broken nose.

"Right. I don't know how you talked me into this, mate." Mac looked around. "And I'm amazed at how you got so many people to show up to this place."

Steve elbowed Mac in the ribs. "I'm paying you. You're my security." He laughed. "And it took a month of arguing my point to get the studio to agree to a premiere up here. Admit it. You're loving it. All the attention, fancy duds. Your profile is going through the roof." He smiled and waved at the cameras, stopping and posing with Jess on his arm.

It seemed like all of the Central Coast was out for the premiere of Steve Ryan's new movie, 'A Step Too Far'. Early reviews proclaimed Steve as the new Eric Bana, which didn't please Steve much. And he hadn't been shy about telling people. Mac had a feeling it didn't please Bana too much, either.

Steve walked up the carpet, Jess on his right arm. Mac trailed half a step behind and half a step to the left.

Mac passed his practised eyes over the crowd. This was the easiest ten grand he had ever made. Steve had shown him some stalker-y letters—someone threatening to sort Steve out. Nothing specific, but enough to justify Steve hiring him. And just in time. Bills were due, and the PI business had been very slow.

Steve shadowed him six months ago, wanting to know what a PI's life was like. It got pretty interesting, and to the actor's credit, Steve had helped him out in a pinch—a couple of times—and had the nose to prove it.

Mac shook his head, a wry smile on his face.

"What's up, Mac?"

Mac kept scanning the crowd. "Just thinking how if someone had told me a year ago I'd be good mates with a movie star, I'd laugh in their face."

"We're good mates? Awesome." Steve's smile was genuine. They entered the theatre and made their way to the reserved seats in the front.

"Good enough." Mac sat to Steve's left, and Jessie sat to the right. Mac leaned over Steve. "Having fun, Jess?"

"Well, it's not kitesurfing, but it'll do." She smiled at Steve. "For now."

The lights darkened, and the curtains opened. Steve looked at Mac and smiled. "At least no ads at the premiere. Remember, when it's over, I've got to do the Q&A with the director, so hang around and keep Jess company, okay?"

The credits rolled, and the house lights rose to rapturous applause, half the audience standing. Steve looked around, smiling. He stood, facing the audience, his back to the screen. He waved and motioned for them to be quiet. He waited until the noise quietened to a dull roar. "Thank you. Thank you very much. If you give us a second, the director, Milo Stefanovic, and I will take your questions."

Mac stayed seated. He waited until Steve left his seat, then shifted to the right and sat beside Jessie.

"How's it going?"

Jessie smiled. "This was awesome. Just brilliant."

He took her hand. "Yeah, the movie was pretty good. I'm talking about you. You had a rough time of it."

She shrugged. "You pulled a rabbit out of your arse, or whatever, and I didn't actually spend any real time behind bars, so it's all good." She smiled and pulled her hand free. "A great life lesson on trust. Who to trust. Who not to trust. When to trust. Now shut up. They're starting."

Mac stood and joined Steve, Milo, and a couple of other actors he didn't recognise. He slid a bit to one side and stayed partially obscured by the curtain. The house lights were up, and the audience looked energised. Steve, the director, and the other actors sat in chairs across the stage. Three people wandered the aisles with wireless mics, waiting to shove them in front of questioners.

Steve tapped his mic and waited for the audience to quiet.

"Thanks, all of you. It's a great reaction to a movie I'm very proud of. Milo did a good job, didn't he?" He clapped along with the audience. "This was one of the hardest movies I've ever made, and I couldn't have done it without Mac Durridge. That's him over there hiding behind the curtain. Get out from behind there, Mac. Mac is a PI from a bit north of here. He agreed to let me ride along for one of the hairiest weeks of my life. I learned a tonne from him. What you see on the screen is me being *him*. One hundred per cent."

Mac closed his eyes and shook his head. "Fuck," he muttered under his breath. He smiled and waved and stepped even further back in the shadows. It wasn't the ideal location to keep an eye on the crowd, but it looked to Mac like a friendly group of people. Easy money.

The Q&A lasted almost an hour. Sequels were hinted at, Mac was called out a couple more times, and he steadfastly stayed where he was. At one point, a cameraman from the local TV station trained his camera on Mac for a good thirty seconds.

Mac took a half step toward him, scowling. The guy pulled his head from the eyepiece, looked at Mac, and backed away.

Finally, Steve stood. "That's it for now, folks. Head out to the lobby and enjoy a drink or two on me. Might be some foods out there, too." He handed the mic to Milo and headed to the wings and Mac.

"You looked completely in your element," said Mac.

"Beats getting beat up for real. I didn't think you were that shy."

"Putting my face in front of the public hinders surveillance of those same people later. How long are the drinks going to last?"

Steve flashed his teeth. "Couple of hours. Max. Keep an eye out, okay? If you'll excuse me, I've got to get Jess before someone else grabs her."

"Jesus, Steve. A little young, don't you think?"

"We're just friends. And, Mac, she's twenty. Makes you feel old, doesn't it?" Steve clapped him on the shoulder, jumped off the stage, and took Jess by the hand. Mac watched her lean into Steve and walk to the lobby on the actor's arm.

He hopped off the stage and followed. He wasn't the only security. The film company had hired a contingent of meatheads to handle crowd control.

He held back until the theatre had emptied, then took a spot in the lobby that afforded him a good view of the milling crowd. Clusters of fans gathered around Steve or the lead actress, some tall blonde Aussie actress whose name he couldn't remember: something or other Bourke.

The crowd was predominantly high-end money. A few bogans who'd won tickets from a radio station contest were holding back in awe, looking like they'd never belong.

One family, a mother, father and daughter, was standing just outside the gaggle around Steve. The parents were pressing forward, and the daughter was hanging back. She scanned the crowd. Mac took a step back in the shadows and focussed on her. She looked like somewhere between a tall fourteen and a skinny sixteen. She had short dark hair and a turned-up nose still with hints of baby fat, barely. She wore a black dress and had a coat draped over her arm. She slowly peeled off from her parents, turned and bumped into a distinguished, middle-aged man wearing a suit that cost, in Mac's estimation, at least a year's rent.

She apologised, said something to her victim, tucked her hand under her coat and continued scanning the crowd.

Mac walked over to her and took her by the elbow. "That was very well executed."

She looked up at Mac. "You gonna let go of me, mister, or am I gonna start screaming rape?"

Mac smiled. "In a crowded room? You must think I'm really talented." He reached under her coat and extracted the wallet. "I almost didn't catch that. You're good. Let's go talk to your parents."

"Who?" She looked genuinely puzzled.

Mac nodded toward the couple, who were getting selfies with Steve. "Those two."

The girl laughed. "I came here on my own. Let go."

Mac pressed a little harder on the pressure point on the girl's elbow. He walked her toward the wallet's owner and tapped him on the shoulder with the wallet. "Excuse me, sir."

The guy turned, a drink in his hand, a smile on his face, enjoying himself.

Mac held out the wallet. "I think you dropped this. The young lady found it."

The guy patted his inside pockets, passing his drink from hand to hand, then took the wallet. "Thank you very much, miss." He one-handed opened the billfold and started pulling out bills. "Let me thank you with a reward."

Mac put his hand over the man's. "Not necessary. She lives to help." He turned away, still with the girl's elbow in his grip. He marched her to the door.

"What are you going to do, mister?"

Mac looked back at Steve and the crowd. He shook his head. "Police station is just around the corner. Steve will be okay for a minute or two."

The girl turned and took a step closer to Mac, bared her teeth and swung a knee at Mac's nuts with all the leverage her lanky legs could muster.

Mac twisted out of the way with limited success. She caught him with a glancing blow. He tightened the grip on her arm and pushed her up against the door frame. "Go home. Get out of here. I'm being paid to take care of what's happening here.

Get out of here, and I'll forget I ever saw you." He spun her to face out the door and gave her a little push. "Go home, and don't come back."

She hesitated, looked at him strangely, then ran away.

Mac watched for a minute to make sure she didn't return, then limped back toward the gaggle around Steve. Steve caught his eye, nodded and smiled.

"What are you laughing at?"

Steve separated from the crowd and put his arm around Mac's shoulders, laughing. "She dropped you like a dirty napkin, Mac. I think I'm paying you too much for security."

"You good? You're all right?"

"I'm great, Mac."

Mac nodded and clapped him on the shoulder. "I'll be over here, in the shadows, watching you." He looked toward the door. "I think you're safe, now."

Steve shook with laughter and re-joined his admirers.

Chapter Two

The house was wedged between two other five-million-dollar homes on the Vaucluse waterfront in Hermit Bay. The backyard sloped down to a jetty poking into Sydney Harbour and a small private beach interrupted by a natural rock pool. To the west, the lights of the Harbour Bridge and the Opera House flickered in the distance.

Vinnie Watson checked his watch and fiddled with his phone. His expensive suit strained against layers of back fat. He shot the cuffs of his shirt and paced his patio. He rechecked the time. It was Thursday now. Twenty minutes in. He adjusted his tie, then removed it, sighing with the released pressure as his top shirt button popped open. He rolled the tie and placed it on the table. He rechecked his watch then heard the quiet murmur of the approaching boat.

Vinnie waited. His security would handle the arrival. It took a minute before he saw his guests.

Prime Minister Lambert slowly walked up the stairs, China's President Lang Ke Shou walking beside him in deep discussion in a suit that looked like it was just put on. A large Chinese security agent walked behind Lang, wielding a large metal briefcase. Lambert looked up as they reached the top of the stairs, saw Vinnie and smiled. "President Lang, this is Vincent Watson. My Chief of Staff. A trusted aid. This is his house. We can talk here in complete privacy. Anything you want to say to me, you can say in front of Vinnie."

President Lang stuck out his hand. "I have heard of you, Mr Vinnie. The Prime Minister has spoken extensively of you and your relationship."

Vinnie held up a bottle of scotch. "Neat, correct? Anything for your man?"

Lang smiled. "You've done your research. And no, nothing for Huang. He'll stand there until it's time to leave. And he speaks no English, so we can speak freely. Honest." He accepted the drink and sat at the table, and motioned for Lambert to join him. "I'm sure we can finish our business tonight." He took a sip of whiskey, closed his eyes and smiled. "Smooth."

Lambert sat across from Lang, glanced at Vinnie and nodded. The Prime Minister placed his elbows on the table and leaned forward. "I think we are close, Lang. Valuation is complete. I'll make sure the approvals for the mine sale get pushed through. The share price is currently at $23.95." He looked over his glasses at Lang. "That's a bit higher than you were expecting, isn't it?"

Lang closed his eyes in thought for a second, then snapped them open. "Over fifteen per cent too high." He shook his head and leaned back. Pushed his drink imperceptibly away from him. "Can not do it at that price."

Lambert smiled and tapped on the table. "Come on, Lang. You know me better than that. I've done it for you before. I'll do it again." He stifled a yawn and scratched at his nose in thought. "You want the share price under $20."

"At least. The lower, the better, obviously, but under $20 gets me there." He smiled. "Significantly under $20 gets me there and puts more in your pocket."

"Yeah, yeah. Well, I can't impact the price of ore on the market. Too much inertia. And you lot are buying it like crazy, which is holding the price up."

"There are other ways."

Lambert nodded and smiled. "Quite right. I think the government may need a new tax revenue stream. A mining tax that significantly cuts into company profits. Some regulatory restrictions will be put on the table. It'll hurt—especially the smaller companies. BHP and Rio will be able to absorb it, but the smaller mines, like the one you'll get, will pretty much kill them. The share price will plummet."

"How fast can that happen?"

"I've done it before. Financial markets were a bit weaker, and it took a week. Just the rumour of the tax will hurt the markets sufficiently. And then I cave into the opposition once your deal is made and kill the bill."

Lang smiled and pulled the drink closer, then raised it. "*Ganbei*. To your everlasting health, Mr Prime Minister. May our relationship have a very long and healthy life."

Lambert raised his glass but didn't drink. "And your end of the bargain?"

"Ah, your patience is known to be short." Lang put his drink down and motioned for Huang. He took the case and gently placed it on the table, swung it around so the clasps were facing Lambert and nodded at him. Lambert opened the case and slowly raised the lid.

The interior of the case was lined with deep red velvet. A flat blue and white dish, the delicate engraving showing its quality, lay nestled in an indentation designed for the artefact. Lambert's hands hovered over it, like he both wanted to pick it up, and was afraid to. "Yuan dynasty? Fourteenth century?"

Lang had moved around to the same side of the table and stood beside Lambert. He nodded. "You have a good eye. It is to your liking?"

"It is. It's spectacular. I thought this was sold at auction in 2014. How did you manage?"

"Let me remain inscrutable. I'm delighted you enjoy it."

"Oh, I do." Lambert closed the case and latched it. "That's worth about six million. The rest?"

"The remaining nine million and change will be transferred to the account we agreed upon when the mine sale is closed."

Lambert looked at Vinnie who stood and retrieved a slip of paper from his wallet. "Different bank," said Lambert.

Lang nodded at Huang who took the paper from Vinnie without looking at it. "I will make the changes to the arrangement. No problems, I hope?"

Lambert glanced at Vinnie, who shook his head slightly. The PM looked back at Lang with a warm smile on his face. "Diversification. Keeping the investments spread around." He looked at his watch. "The hour is late, Mr President, and we have to face the press together in the morning. I will let you go. I look forward to a long and mutually beneficial relationship with both you and your country."

Lang tipped back the rest of the scotch. "I trust, Mr Lambert, that you keep up your end of the arrangement. And if you do, our relationship *will* be long and mutually beneficial."

He nodded at his security and headed down the stairs to the launch. "We can find our way out. I think you two need to talk about things."

Vinnie watched him leave and waited until he was out of sight before he spoke. "That guy fucking creeps me out."

Lambert lightly brushed his fingertips along the top of the case. "That guy is fucking loaded. And when he's happy, I'm happy." He took a deep breath. "The account?"

"The old one is cleared out through a couple of intermediaries and closed out. There shouldn't be a trace of it left."

"Shouldn't?"

Vinnie rubbed the back of his neck. "There isn't a trace of it. It's late, George. You said it. Early morning tomorrow and you still need to get across the bridge."

"I'll sleep on the way over." He clapped his friend on the shoulder. "Retirement is going to be nice, Vinnie. And I'll make sure you get your share of the pie."

"How are you getting back? Chinaman's got the boat."

"He can have it. Cold as hell coming across the water. My driver should be outside your door." Lambert tossed back the scotch and handed the glass to Vinnie. "We'll catch up tomorrow." He corrected himself. "Later today."

Vinnie's phone warbled with an incoming message. He put the glass down and frowned. He opened the message and grabbed the Prime Minister's arm as he was leaving. "Wait." He typed a short message back.

"What?" Lambert glanced at his watch, then at the stairs from the patio into the house. "It's late."

"Your wife has disappeared."

"She's in Vanuatu. You told me that you saw the airline reservations yourself."

Vinnie shook his head. "No, she's not. Didn't make it to the airport this morning. Disappeared off the face of the earth." He held up his phone. "And my guy found this note."

Lambert rubbed his face and took the phone. He scanned through the message and handed the phone back, pale under the patio lights. "Shit. Shit, shit, shit." He pointed at Vinnie. "No cops." His face slid into a stony visage. "Find her, and make sure you clean up any mess you might make on the way. I'll make sure you have whatever funds you need."

Chapter Three

The next morning started early for Mac. He woke up in darkness, bladder pressure serving as his long-time constant alarm clock. His 'bedroom' was a room behind his office. More accurately, his office was the lounge room of his apartment, replete with an old desk, a borrowed iMac and a row of file cabinets.

He pulled on a jumper against the cool dampness of the morning and padded through the dark apartment in silence. He relieved himself and checked his tender nuts. Still attached but showing a little bit of bruising. "Bitch."

He poured a large cup of black coffee at his desk in front of the morning news playing out on his computer. He launched the news channel and sat back, sipping acrid badness.

The top story stopped the cup halfway to his mouth. A young, full-lipped, blonde news anchor looked concerned.

"Prime Minister George Lambert has cancelled his visit to the United States, scheduled for this coming week, where he planned on discussing joint military activities in the South China Sea. A Spokesman for the Prime Minister's office stated that the Prime Minister had to prioritise other, more pressing issues with the arrival of the Chinese President Ke Shou Lang and that he would reschedule the meet-up for later in the year. The Chinese President is in Sydney to continue bilateral trade discussions. A signing ceremony at the Shangri-La Ballroom later this week is being protested, and those protests are expected to increase as the ceremony date draws closer.

"In international news, President Trump—"

Mac closed the browser and poured the coffee down the sink. He walked outside, rested his hand on the cold railing and looked across the street at The Pelican, home of Jess and her parents, who owned the joint. Good food, cold beer and the occasional live band made them the centre of town. He scratched his stomach, thought about the bank balance, closed the door and headed down the stairs.

Halfway down, he noticed the reporter. Linda Carmody. Tall, willowy, with dark, thick waves of hair flowing over her shoulders and a permanent tan. Mac's type if he had twenty fewer years on the odometer. Cute enough, but a lightweight at the local station. He slowed his walk to the bottom, where she waited.

She held out her mobile phone in record mode. "Mr Durridge, Linda Carmody, Central Coast News Network. I'm doing a background piece on the arrest of George Harris, Tom Jackson, the bank robbery they were both involved in and then the subsequent murder of Tom Jackson. All stories in which you seemed to have some involvement. Can I have a minute of your time?"

Mac started laughing before she was halfway through the sentence. "A minute? That's going to take a lot longer than a minute. That's a couple of books worth."

"We can chunk it up into smaller pieces."

Mac looked at the phone in her hand, held up like a microphone. "Miss Carmody, I appreciate your interest. I would love to talk with you about this, but I need to run some errands first. Stop by later, and I'll give you what I can, okay?"

Linda fished a business card out of a holder on the back of her phone case. "Give me a call. Any time, day or night."

Mac took the card and slid it into his pants pocket. "Sure thing." He brushed past her and headed to The Pelican and breakfast.

The difference between Mac's office and the offices of Dawkins and Associates was like the difference between a slice of toast with Vegemite and a five-course meal at a harbour-front restaurant.

Larry Dawkins' office was larger than Mac's entire apartment. And his office was one of dozens. Dawkins had finished a great career in the Australian Federal Police and was well-decorated. He'd parlayed that career into an investigative agency ranked as one of the best in the southern hemisphere. His was the go-to firm for celebrity protection, high-profile divorce investigations and anything else that required discretion, as long as your pockets were deep enough.

Dawkins himself was about half Mac's weight and a half meter shorter. A Ben Stiller to Mac's Vince Vaughn. He sat in an expensive bespoke chair behind a handcrafted marble-topped desk. A small stool supported his feet, his legs too short to reach the floor. What he lacked in size, he made up for in style. A suit jacket hung on a coat tree. His starched white shirt, cuffed with expensive cufflinks, was set off by a pure silk tie, a patterned cranberry red.

The desk phone rang, and he impatiently jabbed the speaker button. "Dawkins."

"Mate, Stevie here. That lady's gone to ground. Her path disappears down the Gong way. It's almost like she wanted us to think she was there. But nada. Nuthin'. Peeled back every cover. She's not here. Hasn't been here in months, by the looks of it."

"I'm not paying you to tell me nothing. If she's not south, where is she?"

"Might be overseas?"

Dawkins chewed on that for a second. "I don't think so. That's not how kidnappers work. They need to be local-ish to make the money transfer."

"So then north or west. East gets too wet, too fast."

Dawkins tapped his pen on his desk for a minute, waiting for the offer. It didn't come. "So, Steve, when you head north, you can probably stop when you get to Newcastle. North of that starts getting too far away."

"Me? Nah, fuck that. I've got active shit going on down here. I can't take the time to drive up there."

"We're paying all your expenses. I'll double the fee."

"I'll tell ya what I said the first time: Ya gotta get the cops involved. The feds. You must know some from your time in."

Dawkins threw his pen across the office. "No fucking cops. How many times have I told you? Not an option. At all. The kidnappers were explicit. Cops equals death. And you keep *your* fucking mouth shut about this, too." Dawkins took a breath and calmed himself. "Triple the fee."

Silence crawled over the line for a few seconds before Steve replied. "It's not the money, mate. I don't like setting myself up for failure. This is doomed to fail. There are too many paths to a bad outcome and only one to a good outcome. I'm not a gambling man. The risk isn't outweighed by any reward you've shown me so far."

"Fine, then. There are others."

"None as good as me. Look, kid, I don't know how you're getting the big jobs, but I don't want any part of them anymore, okay?" A click and three tones indicated a terminated call.

Dawkins sat at his desk, looking at the dead phone. He looked around the office. It resonated with success. He didn't allow the possibility of failure. Thick, plush carpet. Dark wood. Quiet discreteness. He opened his door to the reception area. His wife worked the phones. "Kathy, get me a list of PIs based between Hornsby and Newcastle, would you? Try avoiding the infidelity experts, okay? Want a good, discrete team to run an assist for us."

He closed the door and returned to his desk. He leaned back in his chair, scrolled through recent calls on his mobile and dialled. "Vinnie? Dawkins here."

"Hang on a second." Dawkins listened while background noises receded, and Vinnie returned on the line. "Good news?"

"I'm going to need to expand my feelers."

"You mean extend."

"Whatever. It's going to cost a bit more. It's looking like our target isn't south of us. I need to head north. There'll be travel and accommodation costs I wasn't expecting to incur on top of the regular fees."

"Whatever the fuck. Just do it, Dawkins. Call me tonight with a status update."

Dawkins placed the phone on his desk and leaned back, eyes closed, taking deep breaths to reduce his blood pressure. "Just do it."

"What's that?"

Dawkins snapped his eyes forward and was up. "Startled me, Kath. What ya got?"

"Half a dozen possible. Thin market up there. Want me to set up some calls?"

Dawkins waved his wife aside. "I got it." He scanned the list. "This'll consume the rest of the day for me."

"Dinner at the Clemens' place tonight, remember."

Dawkins shook his head. "Not a chance. I need to close this one out before I do anything else." He sat at his desk with the list in front of him, focussed on the contents. "I'll be out of town this evening. Don't wait up."

"I'll stay and help. I'll give the Clemens a call and cancel."

Jessie re-filled Mac's coffee and popped a hip. "So, is Steve heading back up here anytime soon?"

Mac pushed himself back from the table. "It's not my day to take care of him." He smiled. "I'm sure he'll stop by when he's in the neighbourhood, but I think he's in Thailand shooting a Surf Ninjas sequel."

"Surf what?"

"It's a joke. He's out of town for a couple of months. What did you think of the movie?"

Jessie shrugged. "It was okay. He didn't take his shirt off often enough." She smiled, her brain elsewhere for a minute. "So if you're talking to him, say I said hi, okay?"

Mac nodded and stood, digging bills out of his pocket. He fanned them, pulled a ten and two fives and dropped them on the table. Jess looked at the money and frowned.

"I know," said Mac. "Crappy tip. Money's a little tight. Need to drum up some business; the sooner, the better."

Jess's sense of friendliness disappeared instantly. She cocked an eyebrow, spun on her heel and headed back to the kitchen. Mac waited until she was out of sight and retrieved one of the fives.

He walked out the door with Jess's voice ringing from the kitchen. "I saw that, Mac, you arsehole."

The greasy, albeit very tasty, breakfast sat heavy in his stomach. He stood at the bottom of the thirty-seven steps, rested his hand on the railing and slowly walked up. He reached the top, gave the brass plaque with "Mac Durridge, Private Investigator" on it a soft tap and reached for the door. He stopped. It was ajar. He slowly extracted his handgun from his shoulder holster, gripped it with both hands and kicked the door open.

"FREEZE."

Eight people sitting or standing in his office all stopped talking with one another and turned toward the door. A young, tall, heavily tattooed man laughed. "What the fuck you doing, Mac?"

"Jesus, Nazmi. What the hell? Breaking into a PI's office? That seemed like a good thing to do?"

Mac took in the rest of the office. Gerry and Sue, Jessie's parents, were there. Kaye from the real estate shop down the road, Jenny from the service station, Beryl from the craft shop next to Nazmi's kebab joint and a couple of others he recognised but had no idea what their names were. All of them waiting for him.

Chapter Four

"Is it my birthday? What's the occasion that all of you would willingly break and enter my office." Mac moved Nazmi out of his chair and sat behind the desk. He wiggled the mouse until the screen woke up. "I'm not joining any neighbourhood watch if that's what you're looking for."

Nazmi sat on the corner of the desk. It looked to Mac like Naz was the ringleader. Eight years ago, when Naz was fifteen and Mac was still a cop, Mac had busted him stealing cars. He knew Naz wasn't one of the usual crowd in Gosford, and the kid was scared shitless. Not at all like the rest of the mob he hung with. During interviews, it came out that his old man was already in the slammer for drugs, and Nazmi was a loose cannon. Mac had a come to Jesus talk with him—not really Jesus, given his Muslim upbringing—and put in a good word for him and kept his sentence low and in juvie. Six months later, when he got out, Mac put him in touch with a friend with a kebab shop and got him off the streets. The best investment he ever made. Naz was now a 1.9m, 100 kilo man who, if push came to shove, was on his side.

"So what is it, Naz?"

"Mr Tabeesh to you."

"What? I piss you off somehow?"

"We're entering into a contract. Should be a bit formal, right?" He smiled, pulled an envelope out of his back pocket and dropped it on the desk. The thud signified considerable cash. Mac opened it and ran his thumb across the edges of the bills. Mostly twenties and fifties. He looked at Naz and the rest of the room. "Gotta be at least three thou in here. What's this about?"

They all started talking at once. Mac sat back and waited for Nazmi to get things under control.

When they had quietened, Naz dropped a file folder on Mac's desk. "We've all noticed a sharp increase in inventory loss over the past three months. Two months, three months, something like that."

Mac frowned. "Even you? How does someone rip off you?"

"It's not like they're stealing my fucking kebabs, excuse the French. Soft drinks, water, the extra stuff I sell like crisps, gum, like that. Let me finish."

Mac looked at the seven behind Naz. Some were sitting on his few chairs, others leaning against the walls or the file cabinet. Beryl, pushing seventy, was standing. Mac stood and motioned her over. "Sit in my seat, Beryl. Don't want you to fall over."

"I'm in better shape than you are, Mac," said Beryl. But she took the seat anyway.

Mac picked up the folder. "Finish, Naz. What do you folk want me to do? People usually go to the cops if you're getting ripped off. This is their sort of arena."

"We talked to them," said Beryl. "Individually and in a group. They took notes and did little else. We're taking matters into our own hands. Gerry and

Sue told us what you did for Jessie last year. They seem to have some confidence in what you're doing."

"That's nice of them." Mac smiled at Gerry. "You guys losing inventory, too?"

"Just the stuff you steal, Mac. They asked us for a reference. Thought we'd come along for the talk."

"What about you, Kaye? She stealing houses from you?" Mac smiled. "Sticking them under their jacket and sneaking out?"

"I think she's been squatting in some of my vacancies. Pretty sure, actually."

Mac sat on the corner of his desk. "Well, I'll do some looking around. If you guys can get me the video from security cameras, that'll greatly help." He looked at Beryl. "Yours work yet?"

She nodded. "My grandson installed a real one a few months back." She tapped the folder. "Look in there."

He opened it and spread the contents on his desk. Lists of suspected stolen items, mostly low value but high in quantity, were stacked on top of a couple of pictures. One showed a tall, slight figure in a hoodie, face pointed most of the way away from the camera. The second was closer on the face. Upturned nose with a little bit of baby fat still visible. "Damn."

Mac looked between the two screen grabs again. "Don't bother sending me a video. I know her. Any customers complain about losing their wallet or phone when she's around?"

The room was silent for a few seconds, and then Jenny snapped her fingers. "There was a guy last week. Filled his tank, Seventy-odd bucks. He stood in line and, when he got to the front, claimed he'd lost his wallet."

Mac nodded. "More like her M.O."

"How do you know her?" Nazmi crossed his thick, tattooed arms and leaned in. "Huh?"

Mac dropped the sheets on the desk. "That actor guy, Steve Ryan, had me doing security at his premiere last night. This young lady was cruising for wallets. Had her in my grip."

"So she's been apprehended?"

"No, Beryl, she hasn't been. Unfortunately. If you fine people had come to see me yesterday, she might have been." Mac shrugged. "I was on the job, though. I intercepted her on the job and escorted her out." He scratched the back of his head. "I haven't seen her around here before. How long has this been going on?"

"I told you. A couple of months," said Naz. "Trust me, it took us a long time to get those two pictures. She's good. Very sneaky. Which is why we're here, and you have an envelope stuffed with twenties and fifties."

"She must be. Last night was the first time I'd seen her." Mac picked up the inventory sheets, stacked them with the two photos, slid them back in the folder and handed it back to Nazmi. He sighed. "Give me some timelines. When did you notice her in the shops, and when did you notice the losses?"

Chapter Five

Dawkins crossed another name off the list and looked at the last one his wife had provided. "Malcolm Durridge. Why does that name sound familiar?" He sighed and leaned back in his chair and dialled.

"Mac Durridge PI, Mac speaking. What can I do for you?"

"Mr Durridge, my name is Lawrence Dawkins of Dawkins and Associates. Perhaps you've heard of us?"

"Big firm in Sydney. What would you want with me?"

Dawkins wiped his damp hands with a linen napkin. "We're running an extremely confidential case with tentacles in your neck of the woods. I'm reaching out to get you on board to help us out. The fees will be good and, hopefully, the effort should be light."

"Flattered, really, but my plate is pretty full. Plus, I know a couple of guys you've reached out to in the past, and it takes you an inordinately long time to cover costs. Not interested, thanks." The line went dead.

Dawkins looked at the phone. "Son of a bitch." He pressed re-dial and listened to the call go to voicemail. "The fucker." He slammed his phone down on his desk. "Kath!"

His wife popped her head into the office. "What happened?"

"We need to head up the coast. Full court press."

Kathy narrowed her eyes. "Why this guy?"

Dawkins flicked off the office lights and closed the door behind him. "He just pissed me off. And he's in the general vicinity of where we want to look."

"Lots are." Kath picked up a Yellow Pages opened to Private Investigators and dropped it on her desk.

"Come on. Let's go." He held the front door for her, waiting while she grabbed her coat and bag. "This guy also showed absolutely no interest in the money."

"And that's a reason?"

Dawkins shrugged. "Good as any. I need eyes and legs. He'll do as well as any."

Vinnie Watson sat in a lounge chair on his back deck, sipping on some very old whiskey. He was in a bathrobe, the knot at his waist straining against his gut. His meaty hands dwarfed the glass. He swirled the ice and put his glass down on a glass-topped table. His boss sat across from him, no drink, and by the look on his face, he was in no mood for horseshit.

Vinnie leaned forward. "Mr Prime Minister."

Prime Minister George Lambert scowled. "Vinnie, mate, we've known each other since school. Fuck off with the PM shit. You only do that when you're trying to piss me off, and I'm in a bad enough state." He nodded at Vinnie's glass. "And I'm half a step from day drinking, too."

Vinnie sat back, half a smile on his face. "Right." The smile slipped away. "I've got Dawkins on it."

Lambert stood and loosened his tie. He pulled it through his collar and slowly rolled it. "I don't know what to do, Vin. This is why I've got you as an advisor. You're supposed to help with this kind of crap."

"And I am, mate. Although 'this kinda crap' wasn't in the original brief. You know Dawkins. He's the best there is. Discreet." Vinnie squinted against the sun at Lambert while he paced. "You're not getting soft on me, are you?

"Oh, fuck, I'd stab a rival in the neck at the drop of a hat, but this is different. We need a recovery. No fuck ups. No press." Lambert paced, twisting the tie. "And no money changes hands. I don't care how far we have to go. I'll be fucked if that happens."

"So, completely under the radar." It wasn't a question.

"You're good at that sort of thing."

Vinnie sucked air through his teeth. "A little more delicate than the normal smash and grab."

"Which is why you got discrete help." Lambert shoved the balled-up tie in his pocket. "Recover my property." He paused. "And eliminate those around her. Then bring her home."

"And by 'eliminate', you mean..." Vinnie let the sentence trail off.

"It means what it usually means. Leave a mess or make them disappear. I don't care which. As long as it doesn't come back to me, you or anyone tied to us."

Vinnie stood and walked to the end of the patio, looking over the water to the bridge. "Finding is the first step, and it's the hardest. It's a big-arsed country." Lambert stood beside him, towering over Vinnie by at least 10 centimetres. Vinnie looked up at his friend. "I'm going to be charging you a lot of money."

"As long as you're discrete."

"We're going around in circles here, mate," said Vinnie. He checked his watch. "Don't you have someplace to be?"

Lambert nodded. Grabbed Vinnie's hand and shook it. "Keep me informed at all times. I'll see myself out."

Vinnie watched the Australian Prime Minister walk up the stairs through his house, then scrolled through the contacts on his phone. He heard the limo start and pull away.

Wilson, Dawkins' driver, was turning right onto the M1 off Pennant Hills Road when Dawkins' phone rang. He was sitting up front with the driver, his wife in the back of the BMW SUV. He looked at the incoming caller and put in his earbuds.

"Dawkins here. New news?"

"Boss was just here, pressing. Give me a status update," said Vinnie.

Dawkins glanced in the rearview mirror at his wife. She was busy scanning a file. He lowered his voice. "The shire is clear. Stevie has scoured the area. I'm sure he had his little minions going door to door."

"One quadrant down, three to go."

"Two. The ocean isn't an option."

"Yeah, you're right," said Vinnie. "And I've got contacts in the federal space keeping an eye out to ensure she doesn't end up on a flight out of the country." He paused. "You're in a car. Where are you off to?"

"Up the coast. There's a small but reputable agency about halfway between Gosford and Newcastle. I'm catching up with him this afternoon. On the way back, we'll ping a couple in the west."

"They're discrete?"

Dawkins looked over his shoulder at his wife. "Yeah. Kath is on it."

"The boss was extremely explicit. Maximum discretion." Vinnie paused. "We're private, right?"

"Yeah. Earphones in. Why?"

"When we find her - not *if* - we eliminate anyone and everyone connected to this, and bring her home, all under the radar."

"And by eliminate, you mean..."

"Exactly what you think it means."

Dawkins wiped his mouth. "Fuck."

"Is that a problem?"

"It's a -- skill set I will need to outsource."

"I don't need to know the details. Invoice me. Under the radar means so close to the ground that it picks up dust. Just do it."

Dawkins terminated the call and looked at his phone.

"And by eliminate, what exactly *did* Vinnie mean?" asked Kath.

Dawkins looked at his driver, then back at his wife.

"Oh, Jesus, Larry, relax. If Wilson were going to rat us out, he would have done it years ago. Right Will?"

The driver grunted. "I know nuthink."

"See? Spill it, husband. How dirty will our hands get on this one?"

Dawkins sighed. "Maybe dirty. But always at arm's length." He tapped the driver's arm. "How long, Wilson?"

"Forty-five minutes plus however long it takes to find the guy."

Chapter Six

Emma shrugged her thin coat around her shoulders and slid down the back wall of The Pelican. She rummaged through the canvas shopping bag and pulled out a package of cigarettes. Pangs of hunger wracked her stomach. She clumsily lit the cig, took a deep draw, coughed, and leaned her head back against the wall. She closed her eyes and thought back over the past six months, wondering what she should have done differently.

The final straw in her shit life happened just after Christmas when the house beside hers in San Remo and the one across the street were both raided by the cops on a massive drugs operation. The luck of the draw was the only thing she could think of that spared her guardians' place. She didn't call them parents. They weren't. Her 'mother' was really Anne, a stepmother her dad married when her real mum walked out on them. She was six then. She would have walked herself if she knew what was to come.

Her dad died of a heart attack three years ago, and the man in the house, currently, as far as she knew, was Luke, a meth-head her step-mom had hooked up with. He was freaking the fuck out when the cops were next door. And across the street. She smiled to herself and took another drag. The cigarette dulled the hunger. She'd have some spending money if the fucking ape hadn't intercepted her at the movie thing. She sighed and took another drag.

After the massive drug raid, the adults in her life became the least responsible people in the house. It was like Luke thought he was bulletproof. Traffic in and out of the house increased a tonne, and none of the visitors were members of the Chamber of Commerce. A good number took one look at her developing fourteen-year-old body and figured she was part of any deal they were doing.

She made sure they knew she wasn't. And that caught some beatings from both parental figures.

After the last one, late January, she packed a bag with a few belongings and walked.

It was still warm then. Some school friends let her crash at their place. She drifted north until she ran out of friends. And if she was honest with herself, her friends' parents were starting to get tired of her. She was pretty good at picking up on the moods and feelings of others. It came in handy, that skill.

She'd been lucky with the lifting stuff from people so far. She could tell when people were getting suspicious of her. The guy that nabbed her last night was good.

It was fun when she started. Having no real responsibilities, ditching school permanently, and living off her considerable wits. And wiles. The best part was not having her 'parents' on her back all the time.

Her pocket money ran out after a week and a bit. But that was not really a problem. The stores all overcharged for things, so stealing wouldn't hurt them. She managed to grab and run with pretty much anything she needed. Her long legs helped. She had impressive acceleration.

After a while, she started picking pockets. She had a few rules. First, only people with really expensive shoes. You didn't spend money on shoes - *real* money on shoes - unless the rest of your shit was sorted out.

Second, only in really crowded places. A bump and brush is natural when you're on a crowded train, in a busy shop or, like last night, at a theatre. She had heard about the premiere of *A Step Too Far* happening in Gosford and took the train down. Guaranteed money there. And the fucker had nabbed her. For a few brief minutes, she thought it was over for her - that she'd be in a cell somewhere, and her drug-addled guardians called. She'd have ended up in some juvenile facility for sure. There was no way Anne and Luke would take her back. And no way she wanted to go back. As soon as she left the theatre she grabbed the train back up the coast.

She took another drag and rummaged through the bag. Pulled out a pack of salt and vinegar crisps and started munching on them. A cigarette did only so much for hunger.

In April, she'd started doubting the wisdom of her actions. The temperature started dipping down to the low teens at night and barely into the twenties during the day. A spell of three weeks of almost incessant rain almost drove her back to San Remo.

Almost.

The thought of Luke, with his picket fence teeth and shitty tatts, steeled her resolve to go it alone. Emma ground out the cigarette butt and tipped the bag of crisps back, and dropped the crumbs into her mouth.

"You got anything else to eat?"

Emma jumped and instinctively threw the crisps bag in the general direction of the voice. "Who said that? Who are you?" She stood and pressed her back against the wall, hands clenched in fists by her waist. She peered into the dark. A middle-aged, scruffy-looking man, about her height and weight but three times her age, stepped out of the shadows.

"The name's Barry. Baz. Relax. I'm not going to hurt you. You look starving." He took a few tentative steps toward Emma.

She wrinkled her nose. "God, do *I* smell that bad?"

Barry shrugged. "Hard to say. It's all relative. You run away from home? You look cold, too."

Emma wrapped her arms around herself. "None of your business, I think." She looked around the alley and then started toward the main road.

Barry reached out and grabbed her arm. "Hang on. I won't bite. I've got food I can share."

"Perv." She pulled her arm free.

"Oh, Jesus, girl. You're what, fifteen? Sixteen at the most? Not my bag, darlin'. Look, I'm tough as an old wombat. Not a sexual target for *any*one. And I've been on the streets almost as long as you've been alive. You, on the other hand, are just asking for trouble." Barry clapped his hands together. "You should call your mummy and daddy and tell them you're coming home."

Emma spat on the ground in front of Barry's feet and turned down the alley. She stopped halfway to the main road. The man who nabbed her the previous night was walking down the alley toward her. "Oh, fuck."

"Been looking for you, young lady. You've been pissing off a lot of locals. We need to talk."

Chapter Seven

Emma tried bolting past Mac. He sidestepped, blocked her path and grabbed her by both arms, just firm enough to keep her from getting away. She struggled and tried to free herself, her legs swinging.

"Whoa, miss, calm down. What's your name?" Mac slowly walked her back into the alley. Baz shoved his hands in his pockets and moved out of the way.

"Fuck you. Let go of me before I scream rape."

Mac threw his hands up in the air. "Again, with that? Relax, dammit. Why all the hostility? Don't kick me in the nuts again, or I might not be so gentlemanly."

"You've been following me? How did you find me?"

Mac smiled. "I'm not a huge fan of coincidences. But this is well and truly one. Tell me something. Did you pop down to Gosford just for the movie crowd?" He held up his hands to forestall an answer. "I'm not going to turn you in for that. The only thing I caught you at, well, the fat cat got his wallet back. No harm, no foul, right?"

She glanced at Mac's groin.

"Don't worry about that. You missed."

"Not much of a target. So what are you doing here, then?"

Mac shrugged. "This is not your lucky day, whatever your name is. You've been spotted around here being all klepto-like. Pick-pockety, too. An unruly mob descended on my office this morning, pooling their resources to hire me to bring you to justice."

Emma shook her head. "I don't know what you're talking about."

Mac held out his phone. "You're telling me that's not you?"

She didn't look at the phone "It's not me."

Mac sighed and put the phone back in his pocket. "I'm trying to help you. I could have dragged you off to the police station, easy. You're tall but lanky. You'd probably give me a good fight, I'll give you that, but you would lose." He crossed his arms. "So let's start new. What's your name?"

"Emma Carter."

Mac nodded. "Nice to meet you, Emma. How old are you, fifteen?"

"Almost." She sniffed and wiped her nose with her sleeve. "So what are ya going to do?"

"Jesus. Fourteen? What are you doing on the street? I mean, shit. You're just a kid. Baz here, he's as tough—"

"—As a wombat. And I'm just a little, helpless girl. Yeah. He told me. What do you care?"

Mac looked around. He knocked on the back door of The Pelican. "Come in here out of the cold."

He knocked again, and Jessie opened the door. She stuck her head into the alley, saw Barry and scowled. "He's not coming in, Mac. Scares the customers." She sniffed. "And he smells."

Mac looked at Barry and raised his eyebrows. Barry nodded and slipped back into the shadows. Mac turned back to Jessie. "Just Emma and I, okay? She needs some food. I'm buying." He placed his hand on the middle of Emma's back and gently propelled her through the door and into the restaurant's kitchen. Gerry was standing in front of a floor-to-ceiling refrigerator, taking inventory. He turned when they walked in.

"Mac. Never one to come in the front like everyone else. What can I do for you?"

Mac scratched his chin, looked around and sat Emma at a small, two-seater table. "So, this morning Naz led a posse, including you, to my office looking for a pilferer. You were kind enough to recommend me. Right?"

Gerry closed the refrigerator door and narrowed his eyes. "Is that who I think it is?"

Mac ignored him for now. "And I'm now presented with a strange situation. I'd like your advice."

Gerry sat across from Emma and stared at her face. She stared defiantly back. "It *is* her," said Gerry

"Yeah, I'm me. You're as big a creep as that Barry guy," said Emma. She stood. "I'm outta here."

Mac placed his hands on her shoulders and gently sat her back down. "Emma, you're fourteen, living on the street for reasons I don't understand in the middle of winter. Sit. We need to sort this out."

"Sort what out?" Gerry pointed at Emma. "This is the kid ripping everyone off in town."

"She rip you off, Gerry?"

Gerry stood and slid the chair back into the table. "Besides the point. Your job was to track her down and arrest her."

Mac pressed down lightly on Emma's shoulders. He stopped her from standing. "No, Gerry, I was hired to find her. I found her. Nothing was mentioned about arresting anyone."

"You took their money, Mac. And worked maybe an hour."

Mac pulled the envelope of cash out of his inside jacket pocket. "Give it back to them, will you?" He pulled out the chair and sat across from Emma. "I don't need to know your life history, but I want you to answer a couple of questions for me, okay?"

She grunted but didn't attempt to leave.

"I'll take that as a yes. You're fourteen, right?"

Another grunt of assent.

Mac sighed and looked over his shoulder at Gerry. "Can you bring us both cheeseburgers and chips?"

"Yeah, sure thing." Gerry slapped the envelope of cash on his palm and slid it into his back pocket. "Couple of minutes."

"Thank, Ger." Mac turned to Emma and leaned forward with his elbows on the table. "Do you have any family around here?"

"No." She thrust her chin out, defiant. "I have no family."

"Mother or father?"

"Mum's run off years ago, and dad died. I can handle myself, perv."

Mac ignored the insult. "I'm sure you can. Don't doubt for a minute you'll live through this winter and many more. It's not like it's Antarctica out there. But that's not really the point. I couldn't sleep at night if I knew you were sleeping rough."

"Oh, what, you want me to move in with you? Go fuck yourself."

Mac laughed. "If you were double your age, maybe. I'm not a pedo, Emma." Gerry placed two plates on the table. "Thanks, Ger. Dig in, Emma. You'll think better after you've eaten. You sound a little hangry."

Emma scowled at Mac and attacked the cheeseburger as if she hadn't eaten anything in days. Which, to Mac's thinking, was probably true. He waited until her burger was gone, and her focus was on the chips before he talked again.

"You were stealing some strange shit. What were you going to do with a load of thongs? It's not even their season."

Emma shrugged. "They were there. Easy. Never know what you might need."

"It was stupid."

Emma smiled. "I've still got them. What size are you?" She dipped a chip in tomato sauce and ate it.

Mac wiped his fingers on a napkin. "I'm good, thanks. Back to the problem at hand, now that your stomach is full. Where are we going to put you?"

"Put me like what? An object of some sort? Thanks for the food, but I've got places to go." She pushed back from the table and made to rise.

"Hang on, Emma. This is no good."

"Appreciate the offer, Mac - that's your name, right? But I'm not going to be a freeloader. I can handle myself."

Mac looked at Gerry. He thought for a moment. "I've got a huge favour to ask, Ger. Can you get Sue to join us?"

Kathy Dawkins scribbled a note in her pad, earbuds in, listening intently. "The usual payment. And we'll let you know the targets and location when the time comes. Within the week, though. Thanks." She pulled the bud from her ear. "It's set. We tell them when, who, and where, and they will take care of it. It's going to cost us, though."

"The client will pay." Dawkins looked at the map on his phone. "Turn right on Ruttleys Road. It's a bit faster, and we avoid the lights in Morriset."

Wilson swore and downshifted. "A bit more notice next time, boss." The passengers pitched forward as the BMW rapidly decelerated. "Sorry for that." He accelerated out of the corner, leaving some rubber on the road. "Doesn't save that much time, boss."

Chapter Eight

An old but well-maintained house sat at the southeast corner of Wyee Road and Ruttleys Road. When it was built, some fifty years earlier, it was in a quiet corner of a quiet paddock a few miles outside of a quiet country NSW town. Now, that corner was a massive traffic circle, and traffic wanting to bypass the heavily travelled M1 Motorway streamed past the front door every day.

Bob Collins sat on the porch in a cheap plastic chair, a recently opened beer on an upturned trash bin beside him. He was scrolling through social media on his phone when a black SUV left rubber while going around the traffic circle. He snapped his head up, followed the truck around the corner to the right of the house, and then looked left, checking if anything was following. He watched for a minute, then grabbed his beer and ran into the lounge room.

Doug Collins, Bob's younger brother by six years, was stretched out on the sofa in track pants and a Manly Sea Eagles jersey, snoring lightly with a string of drool connecting his jaw to the cushion.

Bob shook his shoulder. "Dougie, wake up."

"Wha?"

"Get up. Shit. Fuck."

Doug pushed himself up and swung his feet to the floor. "What the fuck are you talking about, bro?" He yawned and rubbed sleep crud from his eyes. He looked at the time on his phone and closed his eyes. He leaned his head against the back of the sofa. "You weren't supposed to wake me for another couple of hours. I'm dead. We shoulda got a third to help us."

"More important shit to deal with." Bob looked toward the back of the house. "And keep your voice down."

"What's going on?"

"I think the Feds are onto us." Bob pressed his face against the venetian blinds and pulled one slat down. "Ninety per cent."

"Why?"

"Why do you think? There's probably an army out looking for us."

Doug sighed. "I know you're older, but fuck, bro, you're not smarter." He belched. "Why do you think the Feds are on to us?"

"A black SUV, like a Ford Explorer or something, multiple antennas on the roof, dark tinted windows, left rubber going around the traffic circle. Headed down Ruttleys."

"So? That's away from us."

"They're in the vicinity, man. We thought this was far from the action, but somehow, they've quartered the area enough to know we're up here somewhere. Too close. We need to relocate." Bob released the venetian and ran across the room to a window on the other side of the house. "They never travel in ones, either. There wasn't one behind them. Maybe I missed one in front." He shook his head. "No, I didn't see any behind them."

"You smoke too much weed, bro. You're paranoid." He lowered his voice and looked to the back of the house. "We're not relocating. It took too long to get here, and we got here completely clear. Logistics are too hard. We're staying put, and you're going to knock off the whacky tabakky." He scratched his stomach. "I need food."

Bob looked toward the back of the house again. "Too bad we can't ask her to cook. She's pretty good."

"Don't be a fucking moron." Doug wiped his hand over his shaved head. The stubble was getting soft. Time soon for another shave. He had an image to maintain. He sighed. "I'm not getting back to sleep. I'll run out and get some food. Chicken?"

"Pizza for me." Bob continued staring out the window. "And stop by the bottle shop and grab a slab."

"Pizza, no beer. We need to stay on our game, mate."

Bob looked away from the window and stared at Doug. His brother was pulling on a jumper. "Right.

No beer. When this is finished we'll be buying the best grog, right?"

"Absolutely." Doug grabbed a set of keys from the table near the door. "Make sure she stays in the back out of sight. And fucking calm, okay? She a bitch to manage if she goes off her nut. We can't afford that. A couple of days and we have the money and we fuck off out of here."

Dawkins' phone warbled as the SUV pulled into the parking lot behind Mac's office. He looked at the display, sighed and answered the call. "About to meet my guy, Vinnie. What do you want?"

"I want to meet your guy, too. You know somebody named Steven..." Dawkins heard paper rustling on the other end of the call.

"Yeah, Stevie. My guy in the Shire. What about him?"

"He's been talking to the press. Vagueness, so far, but edging toward the truth. I don't like that. You haven't used him before, have you?"

Dawkins closed his eyes and scrubbed his hair. "No." He sighed. "I'll take care of it. Is that it? I've got to talk to Durridge."

"I want to meet him."

"I'll set up a call once I've briefed him." Dawkins looked up the stairs to Mac's office. "Give me fifteen minutes."

"No," said Vinnie. "I want to meet him face-to-face. And I'll brief him. Get him to me tonight. And I'll handle this Steven fuck. Leave him to me."

Dawkins looked at his phone, the call now disconnected, and pocketed it. "Well, shit."

Steve stepped out of his ground-floor office in Nowra and locked the door behind him. Another day, another dollar. He hopped in his late 1990s Mazda parked at the curb at the bottom of a hill, and started the engine. While it warmed up he searched on his phone for the number for the local news station. Dialled and waited for the other end to answer.

"Kirk Hanson, K99 news. Who's this?"

Steve put his car in gear and pulled away from the kerb. "Let's keep me anonymous for now, okay?

Maybe I'll let you know who I am later. If you run with this."

"Run with what?"

"Have you seen the Prime Minister's wife lately?"

"Nobody has. She's got the flu bug. Or she's on vacation. Something like that. Why, you've got some conspiracy theory?"

A double dump truck crested the hill and downshifted. Stew pressed the phone to his ear to block the engine noise.

"I'm a private investigator. I was working on a missing person's case and—"

The truck swerved across the centre line and hit Stew's Mazda at speed, crushing the car and Stew so fast that Stew had no idea what hit him.

Chapter Nine

Wilson looked at his boss. "You know where we're going? My GPS is shitting itself. Told me to turn around twice now."

Dawkins didn't look up from his phone. "Keep going. Turn right at the end of the road. Keep an eye peeled for wombats. It's that time of day." He scrolled through links on a search page. "This Durridge guy has gotten pretty good press."

His wife flipped open the file on her lap and read from the summary sheet. "Yup. Ex-cop, PI for the past half dozen years. Busted a cop and bank manager about a year ago. Remember that bank robbery? The inside job? Cleared up a cop killing a bit after that. Ex-cop killing, if I'm accurate. Local rumour has it that he's got a cool mill stashed somewhere—a legacy of the bank job."

"He was part of it? I hadn't heard that."

"He was cleared. Locals wonder, though. Can't use money as leverage if it's true."

Dawkins laughed. "I'll appeal to his civic pride. The Prime Minister's wife is missing. He'll be a key cog in the machine to find her."

"In confidence, of course."

Dawkins rubbed his forehead with the heel of his hand. "For now. Later it won't matter."

Emma wiped up the remaining tomato sauce with her last fry and chewed with her mouth open. "Food was great, but there's no way."

Mac shrugged. "Then I hand you over to the police. Better you stay here." He stood and reached for her arm, then had to duck as the pepper mill sailed over his head. "Jesus."

Emma frisbeed the plate at him. It was a small plate, but it still shattered as it glanced off his head. A couple of the pieces remained stuck in his forehead. Blood poured down his face. He could see Emma laughing through red haze of blood as she ran out the back of the kitchen.

The back door slammed shut as Gerry and Sue ran into the kitchen.

Sue stopped short when she saw the blood on Mac's face. "Oh, my." She grabbed a tea bowl from the counter and handed it to Mac. "There are pieces of plate in there. Be careful." She clutched her hands to her chest. "We need to get you to the hospital. Maybe Jane is working tonight."

Mac pulled a sliver of a cheap plate out of his forehead and gently pressed the towel against his head. "Jane? Hell no. My ex-wife is the last person I want to see tonight. Plasters will do. Jesus Christ. Try to help someone and they do that. It's going to be a pleasure earning that three grand." He dabbed at his head and looked at the towel. It was saturated. "Why does the head bleed so fucking bad?" He pressed the towel against his head and grimaced. "I can't clean this up in your kitchen. Where's the toilet back here? Or do I need to use the one the public uses?"

Gerry led Mac toward the back of the kitchen. "I'll get the first aid kit."

"Give me the fucking money back, Ger." Mac grunted and looked at himself in the mirror over the sink. A bruise was forming above his left eye. Blood was smeared across his face. "I look like the poster for a cheap-ass horror movie made in somebody's backyard."

Gerry dropped the envelope, a packet of sterile gauze and some tape on the side of the sink. "I'll be right back with some peroxide. Make sure you get that really clean. Infected scalp wounds can get very nasty."

"Thanks." Mac slid the envelope into his back pocket. He ran the water hot and used paper towels to dab away the blood from his face. A flap of skin the size of his thumbnail hung over the bridge of his nose. He lifted it into place and pressed hard. "Ugh, fuck."

"That's gonna leave a funny scar." Gerry handed him the bottle of peroxide. "But the ladies love scars, right?"

Mac grunted and soaked a rag with the peroxide. Pressed it against the cut and winced. "Son of a bitch, that hurts."

"Could have been worse. Coulda put out an eye," said Gerry.

Mac taped the gauze to his forehead, dead centre. He looked at himself in the mirror and shook his head. "Fantastic."

Gerry chuckled. "Gonna be kinda hard to blend in for a while."

Sue's voice called out from the kitchen. "Where are you guys?"

"In here," said Gerry. "Patching up Mac."

Sue walked to the back of the kitchen, leading two guests. "Mac, these folks are looking for you."

Dawkins approached with his right hand out and a diet cola in his left. "Malcolm Durridge, I'm Larry Dawkins. We talked earlier. This is my wife and associate Kathy."

Mac dried his hands and slid them in his pockets. "I recognise you. And we barely talked. And my answer is the same. You've wasted a lot of time driving up here. I don't subcontract." He pushed past them into the kitchen. He grabbed a broom from the cleaning cupboard. "I've got broken glass to clean up. Give me a bit of space here, pal."

Dawkins and his wife stepped out of the way and looked at each other, frowning. "No, Mr Durridge, this is a bit more important than I think you think it is."

Mac looked at him for a minute, then started sweeping. "Go home, Dawkins. Nice to meet you, Kathy."

Dawkins drained the cola and tossed the can in a trash bin. He looked at the people in the kitchen. "We need to speak in a more private environment. Your office, perhaps?"

Mac continued sweeping, collecting the shards and dropping them in the trash. "I'll give it to you; you're nothing if not persistent."

Sue took the broom and dustpan from him and put them away. "You should go, Mac. It seems like it's important."

"I'm busy." He touched the gauze on his forehead. "There's someone I need to track down."

Dawkins stepped in front of Mac and looked up at him. "Mr Durridge, I really need to speak to you privately. It'll only take a minute. If, after we've talked, you still want to turn down this job, I'll let you be. But we need to talk in private."

"Five minutes. That's all I'll give you. And you can do it here. Because after we talk, I need to look for Emma the Destroyer."

Dawkins looked at Mac, then at Gerry and Sue. "I'm sorry, no. There are national security implications. Your background as a former member of the police force tells me that you can be trusted, but I don't know these two."

Gerry raised his eyebrows. "What do you mean, 'these two'? We own this place that you're talking in."

Sue stood in front of her husband, hands on his chest. "Relax, Ger. We can step out for a minute."

"No," said Mac. "This is your place. We'll step out." He opened the door to the back alley. "We'll be out here. In the alley. With the garbage."

He held the door while Dawkins and Kathy exited, then closed the door behind them. "So what the fuck?"

Kathy looked around at the dumpsters and garbage, then down at her feet. She grimaced.

"There's a very time-sensitive job we need help with, and word has it you're the guy up here to talk to. Are you?" asked Dawkins

"No. No, I'm not. Sorry to waste your time, folks. Nice talk, though." He stepped to one side and extended a hand to the mouth of the alley. "This way out. Catch you later."

"Wait." Dawkins looked at his wife, then appeared to make a decision. "I need you to come with me to Sydney. Tonight. My client wishes to brief you personally. National security implications." He paused, studying Mac's face. "And I realise this probably doesn't mean much to you, but also tonnes of money." He took his phone from his suit pocket and pressed his thumb on the fingerprint sensor to unlock it. The screen shook and Dawkins swore. He tried twice more, then ended up entering the password manually. "Fucking thing never works when your hands are wet."

Mac smiled and leaned on the back wall of The Pelican and crossed his arms. "National fucking security. Right. Tell me what's this about now or piss off."

Dawkins' wife spoke while he hammered out a text message. "A senior federal minister's wife has been kidnapped, and we need you to assist us with location and recovery," blurted Kathy. She looked at her husband. "Larry, we need to cut through the shit here. Mr Durridge, we can't tell you more than that, per our client."

Mac pushed off the wall. "Okay, first, it's Mac. Second, are you fucking shitting me? I haven't heard a thing in the news."

"Of course you haven't. And hopefully, you never will," said Hawkins. He pocketed his phone. "My wife has said too much. But she wasn't lying. Our client wishes to meet you personally tonight."

"The husband?"

"We will be meeting with Vincent Watson. He's handling this. I just messaged him that we're on our way." Dawkins looked at his watch. "The sooner we leave, the sooner we'll get there."

"Why aren't the police working on this? This, surely, falls under AFP jurisdiction."

"The instructions from the kidnappers were extremely and painfully clear. *Any* law enforcement involvement would result in the victim's slow, painful death. We need to let them believe a ransom will be paid on time while we locate and recover her. And we're running out of time. Are you on board?"

Mac shrugged. "Well, it's sounds a hell of a lot more interesting than looking for a delinquent fourteen year old."

Chapter Ten

Mac followed the Dawkins' across the street to the parking lot. Kathy held the back door of the SUV open. "Hop in."

"What, no black bag over my head? I'm disappointed." Mac climbed in the back seat and buckled the seat belt. Kathy climbed in the other side, behind the driver.

Dawkins climbed in the front seat and turned to look at Mac. "I appreciate this. Wilson will drive you back here after the meeting. Regardless of what your decision is."

"Right." Mac settled back and closed his eyes. "Wake me when we get there."

Mac's head rapped against the glass, and he woke with a start. "Where the fuck are we?" He peered through the SUV window into the dark. Sparsely placed streetlights cast deep shadows. Large, well-lit houses hid behind tall walls.

"You're awake. Good. Almost there."

"Almost where?"

The truck pulled into a driveway and stopped at the gate. The driver pressed the call button and spoke something into the speaker. After a couple of seconds, the gate rolled open, and the truck rolled in, stopping near the front entrance. Dawkins hopped out and opened Mac's door.

The front door opened, and Vinnie stood on the stoop in a bathrobe. The robe hung open, exposing a slab of gut hanging over his boxers. "It's fucking late. Fucking get the fuck in here. You're disturbing the neighbours." He turned about face and walked back into his house.

"He's a bit of a dick," said Mac.

Dawkins grunted and followed Vinnie, with Mac in tow, Kathy bringing up the rear. They ended up on the back patio, overlooking the water. The lights from the Harbour Bridge flickered in the distance. The garish smiling mouth at Luna Park was faintly visible in the background.

Vinnie poured a glass of whiskey and sat at the patio table. He placed his drink on a coaster and motioned for the others to join him.

Mac poured himself a glass before he sat. He took a sip, placed the glass on the table and leaned forward. "I heard about you Vinnie. Hard nut. Serious man. What am I doing here? Something about a kidnapping?"

Vinnie grabbed a coaster and stuck it under Mac's drink. "And I've heard nothing but good about you. But I wouldn't be doing this if it weren't for one of Dawkins' other subbies fucking up. I want to look into your eyes and be convinced you'll do the right thing."

"I'll always do the right thing if the money's right. Why aren't the police involved?"

Vinnie reached into his bathrobe pocket and fished out his phone. He scrolled through his emails until he found what he wanted. "Look at this."

The sender was anonymous. It was sent to Vinnie. The body of the email said: *By now, you know she's gone. The price is $5 million. The slightest inkling that the police, local or federal, are involved will result in her long and painful death. We'll give you until Monday morning to get the money together, then we'll contact you again.*

Mac held his hand out, and Vinnie gave him the phone. "Thanks." He handed Vinnie his glass. "Ice, please? Are there any other communications?"

Vinnie shook his head, took the glass and walked to the bar fridge.

Mac pressed a couple of keys and forwarded the email to himself. "You want to find and recover her without paying the ransom." It wasn't a question.

Vinnie dropped some ice into Mac's drink and placed it in front of Mac. "We'll pay it if we have to, but we prefer to mete out the punishment ourselves. I know some guys."

"I'm not surprised." Mac sipped the scotch. "And who exactly has been kidnapped?"

Vinnie pointed across the water. "She lives at Kirribilli."

Mac's eyebrows shot up. "The Prime Minister's wife? It must have happened a couple of days ago. Why are you talking to me now?"

Vinnie looked at Dawkins and shook his head. "We were working on an incorrect assumption that she was taken south. That didn't pan out. Evidence is mounting that she's gone north?"

"*She's* gone north?"

"She was taken north. You want to know what's in this for you?"

Mac leaned back in his chair. "I'm not sure I want anything to do with this."

A lighter flashed in the dark, and the lit end of a cigar led a shape out of the shadows. "Do it for me."

Mac stood. "Mr Prime Minister."

"Sit down." Lambert sat at the table beside Vinnie and across from Mac. "Here's what's in it for you. Two hundred thou. One hundred now, one hundred when you find her." He snapped his fingers. A heavily muscled man in a well-tailored suit walked out onto the patio with a large duffle bag. He dropped it on the table. Lambert stood, opened the zipper and angled the bag for Mac's inspection. "There's over five mill in here. The ransom. If you can find her *and* incapacitate whoever has her, it's yours."

Mac looked at the bag of money. "Are you fucking with me?"

Lambert shrugged. "It's spent money. I'd rather it didn't go to the kidnappers, but if it does, it does. If you can help me prevent them from getting it, it's yours." He reached into the bag and pulled out five stacks of $100 bills. "$20,000 in each. $100 thou all up. As promised." He rested his hand on the stack. "If you take the job. There'll be no paperwork, and I only deal in cash. What you tell the ATO is completely on you."

"You're the fucking Prime Minister."

"They took my *fucking* wife. You in?"

Mac stared at the cash. "Well, it's awfully tempting. What stops me from taking the cash and doing nothing? I'd be substantially better off financially for literally no work."

"I'm a pretty good judge of character. You aren't going to stiff us. You have a work ethic."

Lambert squinted at Mac. "Besides, this isn't enough money for you to hide, and Vinnie here would find you pretty fucking quick."

"So why isn't Vinnie looking for your wife?'"

"We need to keep some distance. The media finds out about this and the police will get involved and, well, you saw the email."

Mac pursed his lips in thought. He shook his head. "I don't know. The money is compelling, but I have a shred of ethics. I'm not convinced my search will bear fruit. This is a fucking huge country."

Vinnie leaned back in his chair, the metal frame creaking under the weight. "You're not the only one helping us out, Mac. Lots of eyes and ears on the ground." He shrugged. "And most of the state has already been covered pretty well." He placed both hands on the table and stood. "So, deal?"

Mac nodded. "Deal." He stood and stacked the five bundles of cash. "Got a bag I can use?"

Chapter Eleven

Wilson left with Mac in Dawkins' BMW SUV, an hour's drive there and another hour return trip.

"You guys got another way back home, or do you want me to call you an Uber?" asked Vinnie.

Dawkins sat across from his client. He took the bottle and poured himself a healthy two fingers. "Five million? Five point two million, actually? Seriously?"

Vinnie laughed. "Incentive. Closed the deal. It's extremely unlikely he'll see more than he already has." He topped up his drink and tapped the Prime Minister on the arm. "You should split. Not comfortable that you were here for this, actually. You should have deniability. I can handle it from here."

Lambert nodded and pointed at Dawkins. "Total confidentiality, right?" He stood and clapped Vinnie on the shoulder. "You think this Mac guy bought it?"

"Sir?"

"Do you think he'll put his best effort in? And maintain confidentiality?"

Vinnie nodded. "Wouldn't have given him the cash if I didn't. Relax. We'll catch up tomorrow. Get out of here. You've got politics stuff to handle."

Lambert collected his suit jacket off the back of his chair and patted Vinnie on the shoulder. "Tomorrow then." He walked up the stairs through Vinnie's house. A minute later, they heard the Prime Minister's SUV start and pull away.

Vinnie placed both hands palm down on the table. "So, you two, go home. And stop fretting about the cash. He ain't going to see a penny more than he's already got. That'll be enough incentive to find her; we'll take it from there. Stay on top of this guy, though. Okay? And no more hints to the press from anyone. Lock everyone down. We can't have this going wide. Understand?"

Dawkins nodded. "Let's go, Kathy. It's going to be an hour and half, at least, before Wilson is back."

Mac woke, opened his eyes and stared at the stack of cash on the small table beside his bed. He pulled his hand out from under the pillow, wrapped around his .38 revolver. He swung his feet to the floor, placed the revolver on the bedside table and picked up one of the stacks of bills. He fanned the end. "What am I missing?"

He opened the bottom drawer of his file cabinet. Removed the file hangers at the back of the drawer and stacked the bank notes out of sight. He placed some old tax returns on top of the cash, stood up and took an appraising look at the results. Shuffled the tax returns a bit, took one of the stacks of money and pulled out about a quarter of the notes. Covered them up again with the papers. "That'll do for now."

He slid the drawer closed, locked it and scrolled through his phone.

"Alf, Mac here. We need to talk—breakfast at The Pelican. I'm buying. Half an hour." He hung up and headed for the shower.

Alf was sitting in a booth with a cup of tea in front of him when Mac walked into The Pelican. Alf's suit looked like it was bought during the John Howard era and hadn't been cleaned since Gillard's short reign. But he was the best Mac knew. He grabbed two menus from the wait station and stopped in front of Alf. "Outside. We need some privacy."

Alf sighed and levered his copious frame out of his booth seat. "It's fucking cold out." He picked his worn suit jacket off the bench seat and pulled it on, glowering at Mac. He pulled it tight and tried, unsuccessfully, to button it.

"You're getting old, Alf. And you need to lose a couple of kilos."

Alf grunted and followed Mac to a table on the patio. He eased himself into his chair and swore. "I left my fucking tea in there. Hang on a second."

"I'll buy you another one." Mac reached into his pocket and pulled out the wad of notes. He peeled one off and handed it to Alf. "I'm hiring you. Everything I tell you from here on in is protected, right?"

Alf took the bill and disappeared it into his inside suit pocket like a seasoned magician. "What have you done now?" He nodded at the pile of notes in Mac's hand. "That's more cash than you've had on you at any one time since I've known you."

Mac folded the bills and stuffed them back in his pocket. "This is all legit cash. I think. That's why we need to talk." He smiled at Alf and opened his menu. "Whatever you want. My treat. Oh, and this is just a drop in the bucket." Mac motioned for a server. "You know what you want yet?"

The server arrived, and Alf and Mac ordered breakfast.

Mac watched the server leave, then turned back to Alf. "Okay. The money."

"Looked like a couple of grand in your pocket."

"It's about five, actually."

Alf nodded in appreciation. "That's a good chunk of change. What's the story?"

Mac leaned forward. "Five *is* a good chunk of change. A hundred is even better, right?"

Alf stared at Mac for a few seconds, incomprehension furrowing his brow. "A hundred grand? Jesus Christ. What's going on?" He sat back in his chair. "Fuck. Do you want me to launder it for you? You hit the numbers?"

"My friend, this is why we're here. According to my new client, this is a down payment. The down payment is a fuck of a lot of money. The full amount..." Mac made an explosion sound. "...blows my mind."

"You're my client now. Full confidentiality. What's the case?"

Mac leaned forward and lowered his voice. "The Prime Minister's wife has been kidnapped, and I'm part of the team looking for her. The cops are not to be involved, or extreme pain and gruesome death to the lady, and I get the distinct impression that the kidnappers will end up as chum."

Alf looked around. "What the fuck? Jesus, man. How in the hell did you get involved with this? How does the PM know you?"

"Oh, he doesn't. Dawkins needs eyes and feet up here. My name was apparently in his directory. He drove me down to visit *his* paymaster yesterday. Some Guido name Vincent Watson."

The server arrived with their food. Steak and eggs for Alf and Eggs Benedict for Mac. They waited while she placed the food and cutlery and left before they spoke. Alf pushed his plate away and sat back. "Vinnie is the PM's Chief of Staff. In reality, he's his fixer. A very powerful man." He sipped his tea and gently placed the cup back on its saucer. "You're right about the chum part. What's the ransom if they're willing to part with a hundred grand for you?"

"Five mill."

"And you are convinced it's real?"

Mac frowned. Played with his egg for a minute. "What do you mean?"

"You see a ransom note or hear a tape? Anything like that?"

Mac nodded and swallowed a mouthful of breakfast. "An anonymous email. Deliver the money on Monday. More instructions to follow."

Alf pulled his plate closer and cut at his steak. "I wouldn't want to be in the kidnappers' shoes. Vinnie doesn't fuck around. So the hundred was a down payment on finding her?"

Mac nodded. "And another hundred when I find her." He smiled and pointed at Alf. "You haven't heard the best part. If I manage to bring the kidnappers down, feed them to the chum machine as it were, I get to keep the ransom."

Alf's eyes narrowed. "Be careful. I thought the hundred was too good to be true. Over five million is insanity." He sliced off another piece of steak and thought while he chewed. "So, what are your next steps?"

"That's why you're here. I need a brain to bounce some things off of. You haven't heard anything about the kidnapping?"

Alf shook his head. "The media has been pretty consistent with the story that she's on vacation. I can ask around and see what I can find out."

Mac tapped his fingers on the table for a moment in thought. Then he shook his head. "Don't actively look for anything. Keep an ear out, but stay out of it. You're right. Vinnie isn't someone to cross."

Chapter Twelve

Cameron aspired to a career in footie, and while he was fast enough and tall enough, he didn't have that small missing ingredient that would propel him to greatness. Which was great for Mac. Because Cameron was a computer genius.

Mac sat in his desk, looking between his computer and the bottom drawer of his file cabinet. He'd made his second cup of coffee since he'd returned from breakfast. He checked his watch. "Fucking hell, Cameron, where are you? I thought you were fast."

He picked up his phone and redialled the number. He held the phone to his head and moved it slightly away from his ear. He could hear the ringing outside his door. He hung up as Cameron entered.

"I'm sorry, Mac. I had to finish my workout. What do you want me to do this time?"

Mac tapped the spacebar on his keyboard, waking the monitor. "I've got an email here. The contents are strictly confidential, okay? I'm paying you $100 an hour for your discretion. Do you understand?"

"A hun-hundred dollars an *hour*? For real?"

"Yes. I want you to see if you can trace where this email came from. Look at the IP address or whatever it is you do. Is that possible?"

Cameron nodded. "Possible, yes. It might take me a little while to trace it back if any proxies were used."

"Any what? Never mind. I wouldn't understand." Mac pulled the folded money out of his pocket and counted off eight bills. "First day in advance. Eight hours. Keep working on it until you find something. Call me if you do."

Cameron took the money and stared at it. "Wait. What? Is this for real?"

Mac clapped him on the shoulder. "I need to hit the road and start door-knocking, Cam. Yes, it's for real. Do your computer thing. Call me when you've peeled back the digital curtain."

Cameron folded the money into his wallet and sat in front of the computer. "Shouldn't take long. I'll probably owe you money back."

"Jesus, kid. You're too honest. Minimum one day, okay? Take your time. Make sure."

Cameron nodded. "Yeah, sure. I'll triple-check. What will you be doing?"

"Missing persons is usually a lot of legwork showing pictures of the person in question. Can't do that this time. Confidentiality issues. I need to attack it from the other side." Mac pulled on a jacket. "I'll be driving around, talking to people. Call when you find something."

Cameron scanned the email. "Holy shit. Hang on, Mac. Is this what I think it is?"

Mac stopped with his hand on the doorknob. "Strictly confidential. Right?"

Cameron exhaled a deep breath. "Fuck."

"Exactly, kid."

Mac sat in his car for a minute, then took out his phone and called his office.

"Durridge Investigations. Mac isn't in. Can I take a message?"

"Shift of priorities, Cam. Before you start digging into the email, check all records in the area for short-term leases, vacant properties, or any place kidnappers might be holing up. And dig up some recent photos of the wife and send them to my phone."

"Should be pretty easy to find pictures of her. You could do it on your phone."

Mac laughed. "You can do it a hell of a lot faster than I can. Thanks." He pulled out of the parking lot, and his phone rang.

"Mac speaking."

"Dawkins here. How's it going? What's your progress?"

"Hang on a sec." Mac plugged his headphones in. "You still there?"

"Where would I go? Give me an update."

"Fuck, man." Mac looked at the time on his dashboard. "I got home less than twelve hours ago. And I had to sleep. Give it a minute or two."

"This is a very time-sensitive operation, Mac, and you know that. Are you the right guy? I thought you were the right guy."

"I'm the right fucking guy. Actively working on it. Do you know how hard it is to find somebody without actually asking people if they've seen her?"

"Doesn't sound like you're the guy. Look, forty-eight hours. That's it. So I'm going to start looking for someone else to do this, and if there's no measurable progress by tonight, say twelve hours from now, then the someone else is going to get the job." Dawkins paused. "And we'll be retrieving that money we've given you."

"Hey, fucking hell-" Mac looked at his phone. Call disconnected. He took a deep breath and exhaled slowly. "Well, shit." His phone beeped. A message from Cameron with three photos. Two group shots and a single of Cheryl Watson, wife of the Prime Minister and current kidnap victim. He cropped the single to get a headshot and made it his home screen. "Best get to work."

Bob stirred and sat up on the sofa. He stretched, yawned and scratched his stomach. "Doug, I need food." He sat up. The lounge room was empty. He looked back towards the bedroom and slowly stood. He walked barefoot, quietly, to the lone bedroom and tested the door. It was locked. He took a deep breath, padded into the kitchen, and started the kettle.

The house was small but clean. Doug had forced the back door open and wedged it shut once they got in. They stayed up front to keep an eye on traffic, and she was stowed out of sight in a back bedroom. She didn't like it, but tough fucking luck, thought Bob. His stomach growled, and he looked at his watch. "Where in the fuck are you, bro," he muttered.

The front door opened, and Doug entered with the smell of breakfast. "You hungry?"

"Fuckin' right. Where the hell have you been? I was getting worried."

"There's a mum-and-pop place in Wyee. Bacon and egg on toasted Turkish. Smells good, right? Turn off the kettle." He placed a cup holder with two coffees on the counter.

"You paid with cash, right?"

"Yeah, yeah. You don't have to keep telling me, mate," said Doug. He tossed a bag at his brother. "Your turn next time. For lunch. Don't go to the same place. Avoid franchises that probably have security camera systems."

"Yeah, yeah. You don't have to keep telling me, *mate*." Bob unwrapped the breakfast sandwich and inhaled deeply through his nose. "Damn good smelling. They probably make a great burger."

"Later, maybe. Not this trip." Doug popped the lid off his coffee and sipped. Winced. "Their coffee is shit. I'll turn the kettle back on." He nodded toward the back of the house. Reached into the bag of food and pulled out a third roll. "Take this back to her, okay? Make sure she eats. We don't need her weak if we have to bug out of here."

Doug spooned ground coffee into a plunger pot they had found in the cupboard and listened to his brother's muted voice in the back of the house. The voices were raised a bit, and then the door was slammed shut. Bob came into the kitchen shaking his head.

Doug watched him while he poured the boiled water into the coffee pot. "Everything okay?"

"This is a fucking nightmare."

Chapter Thirteen

Barry sat, his back leaning against The Pelican's patio railing, sun on his face, eyes closed, soaking up the last remaining vestiges of heat from the noon sun. Same shit, different shovel. The middle of another Australian winter. He had only dim recollections of living in an actual house. Twenty long years ago. A couple of bad financial decisions exacerbated by a crippling alcohol problem was his undoing. Sydney was too rough. He had scars and, long ago, broken bones that ached this time of year.

A shadow passed between him and the sun, and he shivered and opened his eyes. The girl was in front of him. "You're blocking my heat."

Emma snugged her coat tight and sniffed. "What's the deal with this place? I need to get some food. I can't get away with anything around here anymore."

Barry stepped closer and looked closely into her eyes. "You sniffing 'cause you need drugs?" Emma recoiled, and Barry shook his head. "Nah, you don't look like it. Why the fuck you on the street, young as you are?"

She turned away and looked at the moored boats. She sniffed again. Snugged her coat tight again.

"You don't wanna talk, you don't gotta talk," said Barry. "None of my business."

"What about you? How long have you been homeless? And why?" Emma leaned against the railing and looked down at Barry.

"How long? I can't remember when I wasn't." Barry shook his head. "I never did get much of a chance at the best of times. And I fucked it up even worse than usual. I'm a hard nut. Don't worry about me. You, you're what, fifteen? You should be having sleepovers talking to your girlfriends about Harry Styles and Tay Tay. Not bumming with an old drunk like me."

"Yeah, whatever. That fucking PI is looking for me, so I can't grab anything from the shops. All eyes peeled for little old me."

"Mac's an okay guy. Always good to me." Barry nodded toward The Pelican. "He was going to talk them into taking you off the street until you sorted yourself out. And I know Ger and Sue. They'd do it, too. It wouldn't take much convincing at all. They're good people." He shrugged. "Then you painted Mac's face with his blood, and they're a little less inclined." He nodded. "But Mac's a good guy, still and all."

"No such thing. If you see the PI, tell him I've fucked off back to Sydney."

Barry nodded over her shoulder. "Tell him yourself."

Emma turned and saw Mac approaching, phone in his hand, determined walk, plaster in the middle of his forehead. She looked over her shoulder. Water. Nowhere to go. "Fuck."

"Language, young lady," said Mac. "You and Baz best mates now?"

"I was just leaving." She looked at the plaster on his forehead. "Sorry for that." A small smile crept onto her face. "You look like an idiot."

Mac touched the plaster with his fingertips. "Right." He stuck out his hand and stopped Emma from leaving. "Hang on." He held out his phone. "I'm going out on a limb here, but you two are essentially invisible. I need to find this woman, but not tell anyone I'm looking for her."

Emma didn't look at the proffered phone. "Why should I help you?"

Mac pointed at his forehead. Emma crossed her arms and stared at him, jaw set.

Baz pulled himself to his feet and took the phone, squinting at the picture. "Hey, that's what's her name, the PM's wife," said Baz. "She's missing?"

Emma shook her head. "He's fucking looking for her, idiot."

"Really, Emma. Language."

"Fuck you, Mac. If you're not taking me to the police station, I'm pissing off."

Mac held up a hand while he dug in his pocket with the other. "I have a deal for you. And I will have to trust you to hold up your end of it." He handed hundred dollar notes to Baz and Emma. "Get around town. Get an Opal card and ride the bus. Poke your noses in cafes and libraries. Be nosy. You're both essentially invisible. See if you see her anywhere. Get word back to me as quickly as you can."

Barry folded the bill and slid it into his pocket. Emma looked at it, then back at Mac, then at Barry. "For fucking real?"

Mac sighed. "For fucking real. There's more where it came from. And I know there's nothing stopping you from pissing off with the money. But there *is* more where it came from. Find her, let me know where she is, and I'll double that."

Emma reached for his phone. "Let me see her again."

Barry handed her Mac's phone and slid his hands in his pockets. She held the phone with both hands, her thumbs flying.

"What are you doing?" asked Mac

She looked up. "Sending the pics to my phone. Duh."

115

He looked at Emma's thin frame and shivered. He pulled another bill out of his pocket. "Go get a warmer coat. That thing is barely warm enough for spring and it's the middle of winter."

Emma handed Mac's phone back and tentatively reached for the bill, stopping short of taking it. "What is it you're expecting me to do for this?"

"Buy a coat. Keep an eye peeled for the lady." Mac smiled. "Nothing more. You're twenty years too young for me, honey. And too skinny."

"Plus, she's like not legal, Mac," said Barry.

"Plus that. I've got to do my own digging. Back here at sundown, and I'll buy you both dinner, and you can tell me what you found."

Dawkins pulled into the parking lot behind Mac's office and sat in the car for a second, letting it idle. He scrolled through his phone, found Mac's number and dialled. Then he hung up as he saw the detective walk around the corner and start up the stairs to his office.

Dawkins opened the car door and stepped out. "Mac." He closed the door and trotted up to him. "Hey. Thought I'd stop by and see how things are going."

Mac continued walking up the stairs to his office. "You micro-manage everyone? Go back to your office. I'll have her by this time tomorrow."

Dawkins grabbed him by the arm and dodged a swinging elbow.

Mac steadied himself on the stairs. "Sorry about that. Habit." He turned and stood a couple of steps above the shorter Dawkins. He looked down on him. Literally and figuratively. "Come by for lunch tomorrow, and I'll give you a map of her whereabouts. But leave me alone until then. I don't work well with people breathing down my neck. Deal? Or do I give you the money back and let you figure this shit out for yourself?"

Dawkins looked up at him. He pursed his lips and scowled, and tried to look tough. Finally, he pointed a finger at Mac and said, "Tomorrow. At the place across the street. Noon." He turned on his heel and returned to his car. "Or you're out, and I take the cash back."

Mac waited until Dawkins' car pulled out of the parking lot, then continued up the stairs to his office. Cameron was still at Mac's desk, working on something on the computer.

"Any luck with the email?"

"Maybe. There are a couple of extra sets of headers in here that I'm trying to decode. It bounced around a bit."

'But you'll be able to do it?"

Cameron shrugged. "Probably. A bit harder than I've worked on before, but not impossible. Might take me a couple more hours at the rate I'm going."

"Any luck with the vacancies in the area?"

Cam looked up and placed his hands on top of his head. "Oh, shit. I totally forgot. Was that important?"

"No big deal. Get some lunch, kid. You can afford it. I've got to make a couple of calls."

Cam stood from the desk and stretched, almost reaching the ceiling. "No worries, Mac. Be back in half an hour."

"Appreciate it."

Mac grabbed a beer from the fridge and searched for local real estate on his phone. Found what he was looking for and called.

"Green Real Estate, Kaye speaking. How may I help you?"

"Kaye, Mac here. How are you and Jim doing?"

"We're doing great. Are you looking to upgrade from your—well, I'm not sure what to call it."

"It's my multi-functional office, and no. The rent is unbeatable. I wanted to talk to you about something you said yesterday about that girl squatting in your vacant properties."

"You've found her?"

"Found who?" Mac sat at his desk, puzzled.

"The girl. The one we hired you to find. Did you find her yet?"

Mac leaned back and expelled a held breath. "Right. Still looking. It's pretty fucking cold out. I thought she might be holed up in one of your places. Hoping you'd drive me around to some of them, point out the ones I should be keeping an eye on."

He heard a sigh on the line. "I'm doing your job for you now? Do I get my share back? Never mind. I'll do it. I'll stop by your place in five minutes. But meet me downstairs. I'm not climbing them again."

"Thanks, Kaye. Much appreciated."

Chapter Fourteen

Mac stretched his legs as much as he could in the small car. He tried racking the seat back farther, but it was at its limit.

"You make good money, Kaye. Why don't you upgrade your wheels?"

They rolled up to the fifth of six addresses, and Kaye turned off the ignition.

"I'm chauffeuring you around, and you're complaining about the ride?" She levered herself out of the car and stretched. "Don't know what you're expecting to find out here. We're miles from town. Surely, that young girl wouldn't have walked all the way out here."

Mac stood at the kerb and looked at the house. It was a two-story brick house with a paved driveway. A single-car carport looked freshly painted. The windows were bare—no curtains. The interior was dark, and the house looked cold and vacant.

"You want to look inside?" asked Kaye. She fumbled through a ring of keys. "Doesn't look like there's someone in there, if you ask me." She marched up the walk and unlocked the door.

Mac followed her in. He wrinkled his nose. "Kinda stale in here, Kaye. Been empty long?"

Kaye looked around the vacant house. "A few months. I think there are a couple of applications in for it, though." She shook her head. "The girl isn't in here. One more to go.

They piled into Kaye's car, the suspension sagging under their combined weight. Kaye looked at the list. "One last one."

"Nothing else you know of in the area that might be vacant?"

Kaye frowned and looked through the list again. "No. This is it." She dropped the list on the centre console and put the car in gear. "A couple of minutes from here. Wasting your time, I think."

Mac picked up the list and scanned through it. "There are only six vacancies you know of?"

"Tight market, small town."

"Forget about what I said about your car. I don't know how you make a living doing this."

Kaye grunted and rolled to a stop on the side of the road. She pointed across the street at a shabby-looking house. A short gravel drive led to a carport that looked like it was a stiff breeze away from collapse. A small child's swing set was visible in the backyard through the back of the carport. Three unpainted wooden steps led to a small porch, fronds from a dying palm tree draped across the rusty awning over it. And a sea turtle of some sort framed a peephole on the poorly painted front door.

The house stood in the middle of a large lot. Across the street was bush, and to the left, or north, of the house was a paddock. Cows were grazing on the far side. The house had the feeling of a long-neglected farmhouse, abandoned after a particularly harsh bankruptcy.

"That's the last one. It's for lease. Probably will be for a long time. I think I'm going to drop it off the list. The owners aren't willing to put any money into it. And I can't move it at the price they want." Kaye looked down at her property folder. "I think that's all." She cracked open her door. "Want to look?"

Mac kept his eyes trained on the house. A curtain fluttered in the front window. He glanced at Kaye, but she didn't notice. "Thanks, Kaye. I appreciate it. There is no need to look inside. You can take me back. I'll let you know if my search produces anything in any places you're trying to move." He glanced at his watch. "It's getting late. I've probably hurt your business. What do I owe you?"

She pulled from the kerb and looked at Mac with a smile on her face. "Oh, honey, you don't have to do that."

"No, really. You could have just sent me a list of addresses." He dug into his pocket, glanced at the bills and handed her three hundred. "For your time. And fuel for the car."

"It's a hybrid. I fill it up on the first of the month, whether I need to or not." She snatched the bills. "And this hardly pays for my time, but thanks for the gesture." She pulled ahead and turned right at the roundabout. "So what's your next step?"

Mac watched the house as they rounded the corner. He had a pretty good vantage of the backyard. And the old black Holden Statesman parked behind the house. He turned and faced the front as Kaye barrelled down Ruttleys Road. "My funeral arrangements, if you keep this speed up." She stretched the suspension, crossing the bridge over the train tracks. "And after that, I'll poke around some of the places you showed me a little bit closer." He grabbed the handle above the door as she cornered. "Assuming I live that long."

Mac thanked Kaye and escaped her car in front of his office. He trotted up the stairs to an ajar door again. He eased it open with one hand. "Who is it this time?"

He pushed the door all the way open to find Emma sitting at his desk. "You." She was wearing a new, warmer coat and had her feet up on his desk.

Mac glanced at the file cabinet, the bottom drawer secure and closed, and swept her legs to one side. "Keep them off the desk. How long have you been here?"

She shrugged. "I don't know. Half an hour or so."

"You been snooping in my office?"

She shook her head. "Just nice to be out of the cold." She snugged her new coat tight.

"You pick locks now?"

Emma stood. "You left the place unlocked, brainiac. I better go."

"Where?"

"Around." She walked slowly to the door.

"Oh, Jesus. Come with me. We'll get something to eat."

"I could eat."

Mac held the door for her and followed her out, making sure the door was locked behind him. "It automatically locks, Emma. You picked it."

"I don't know what you're talking about."

They crossed the street, and Mac held the door to The Pelican. "Get in there. Find a booth. I'll grab menus."

He waited until she sat then proceeded to the wait station. Jess was at the register. "Your parents here?"

"Always. In the back. Why?"

Mac picked up a couple of menus. "Ask them to stop by in a few minutes. I need to talk to them."

He waded through the crowded restaurant and found Emma sitting in a corner booth. He dropped a menu on the table and sat across from her. "So, a lock pick, pickpocket and a bit of a klepto. And only fourteen."

"Almost fifteen." She smiled.

"You're quite the accomplished thief." He opened his menu. "The bacon cheeseburgers are out of this world. And Sue makes a homemade strawberry shake that's so thick you almost need a spoon."

Emma flipped the menu closed. "So I don't even need to look." She crossed her arms and sat back in the booth.

Mac cocked his head. "Damn, I'm glad I never had kids. Order what you want. I was just making a suggestion." He closed his menu. "But I'm getting the cheeseburger."

Jess appeared at the end of the table. "Ready to order?"

Mac looked at Emma. "I'll have the bacon cheeseburger and your mum's strawberry shake." He handed his menu to Jess.

Emma closed hers without looking at it and handed it to Jess. "Same here."

"Cool. They'll be ready shortly." Jess tucked the menus under her arm and headed back to the kitchen.

Mac looked at Jess and opened his mouth to say something when she interrupted.

"Don't say it. It sounded good. And I'm starving."

"You could put a bit of meat on your bones." Mac leaned forward, his arms on the table and his hands clasped together. "Sue and Gerry are good people. You need to reconsider staying here."

"They don't want me. They've got enough problems."

Gerry approached the booth and slid in beside Mac. Sue sat across from him. Beside Emma.

"What did you order?" asked Sue.

Emma nodded toward Mac. "What he's having. Apparently, I can't think for myself."

Mac shook his head. "Sue, Are you sure about this?"

She reached across the table and took her husband's hands. "Gerry and I talked about it. I think it's horrible that Emma needs to live on the street."

"Don't I get any say in the matter?"

Jess arrived with the milkshakes. "Burgers in a minute." She looked at her parents. "Everything okay?"

"We'll know in a minute," said Gerry.

Jess looked at Emma, then nodded. "Okay. Let me know. Back in a minute with the food."

Emma sucked hard on the straw and took a mouthful of milkshake. "So what, you expect me to just move in here? Just like that?"

"We're extending an invitation. We have an extra bedroom. We'd expect you to help when it gets busy around here." Sue sat sideways in the booth. "I'm a really good judge of people. And if Mac says you're worth it, then I believe him. If you stay out on the street, it will only get worse. Not much chance of getting better. What do you say?"

Emma looked at Mac, suspicion playing across her face. "Let's see what the cheeseburger tastes like before I decide."

Mac tapped the table. "Good enough." He nudged Gerry to get out of the way. "I've got to run an errand. I'm pretty sure she'll be able to eat both burgers. I'll pay for them on the way out." He held up his hand to forestall an imminent objection from Sue. "No, I insist."

Chapter Fifteen

Mac parked in the lot of a small market around the corner from the last house Kaye showed him. He locked up and walked along the shoulder of the road opposite the house until he found a vantage point that obscured him but allowed him an unobstructed view of the front and south side of the house near the carport. There was no other way for the car to leave. A fence ran along the north side, and the back extended out through a paddock that the Statesman couldn't traverse. A Jeep, maybe, but not the car.

He snugged his jacket around him and crouched down in the underbrush. A shallow run-off ditch gave him a bit of cover, and the grass and brush rarely tended by anyone from the municipality made him virtually invisible. An old railway tie sloped into the ditch. He dragged it up and placed it parallel to the road at the top as a resting point.

He knew someone was in there. The car gave that away. The fluttered curtain sealed the deal.

He rubbed the lenses of his binoculars with his shirt tail and squinted through them, adjusting the focus and zoom until the field of view was constrained to the front porch and the carport to the right. He settled himself prone on the sloped ditch, elbows on the railroad tie, glasses to his eyes and settled in for a wait.

Which turned out to be a short wait. The sound of a car starting was followed by the black nose of the Statesman easing through the carport and resting on the road before it turned left out of the drive and sped into town. Mac got a quick glance at the man behind the wheel but not enough of a look to recognise him. But it was definitely a him. Not a Cheryl.

He trained his glasses on the windows for a while. The curtains stayed still. Nobody looked out.

He took a deep breath, hung the glasses over his neck, grabbed the tie and ran across the road. He placed the tie across the drive, blocking the car's entrance, ran back to the brush, and slid down into the ditch. He put his glasses back up to his face and watched.

The driver would have to get out of the car to move the tie when he returned, or he'd need to call someone inside the house to move it. Either way, it was good. Either way, he got eyes on at least one of the kidnappers.

He watched the house for a few minutes. He thought about it for a bit, lowered the glasses and rolled over onto his back. The tie was the trigger. He'd hear it scrape on the gravel drive when it was moved, or he'd hear the car return and stop. Not necessary to watch all the time. It was killing his neck.

He took out his phone, put it on silent, and texted Cameron, *"How's it going with the email trace?"*

"I thought I was almost there, then noticed the path I was following eventually looped back to the location that sent it to you. I must have been doing it wrong. Sorry. Starting from scratch. Still kinda new at this."

Mac scratched his jaw. Sat up and looked across the street at the house. He typed out a message. "*Never mind. Go home. Take another crack at it tomorrow. I'll give you a call when to show. Same rate. $800 a day.*"

"*No can do. I got a job starting tomorrow with an audio-video company. Big thing coming up after this week that I'll be working on. Sorry.*"

Mac read the message twice. "*You're giving up a hundred an hour for a cheap-arsed gig with some AV company?*"

"*It's a career, Mac. Sorry. Something at the Shangri-La. Kinda excited about it.*"

"*Okay. Thanks for your help. I might have someone else who can help. Print everything you've got so far and leave it on my desk.*"

"*Sure thing. Good luck.*"

Mac locked his phone and slid it into his pocket. He heard an approaching car, rolled to his front and squinted through his glasses. The Statesman crunched across the gravel and stopped at the tie. The driver's door opened, and the man got out. At the same time, the front door of the house opened and another man stepped out.

Mac zoomed the view and looked at each of them, one at a time, with their heads filling the field of view. Switched between them, holding the image for five seconds each to memorise, then back to the other for five seconds. They looked familiar, but he couldn't place them.

After a couple of switches between the faces, it dawned on him that they were no longer looking at each other as if they were having a conversation. They were both looking across the road. Directly into his binoculars. Then, they both started walking across the road. Directly at him.

"Fuck."

Chapter Sixteen

Mac stood, glasses hanging around his neck. "Gents, you lads see my dog anywhere? He ran into the scrub. Afraid he might have run across a snake."

They stopped a couple of paces in front of him. One was half a head taller than the other, but by Mac's eyes, they were related. "You guys cousins? Brothers?" He stuck out his hand. "I'm Mac. What's your name?"

The taller one shook his hand. "I'm Doug. This is my brother Bob."

Bob smacked his brother on the arm. "Shut the fuck up, man."

Doug gestured over his shoulder with his thumb. "Why'd you put that across the drive?"

Mac peered over the tall man's shoulder. "What, that tie? I think it's always been there. Look, lads, if you haven't seen my pooch, I've got to go. He's around here somewhere."

Bob stuck his arm out and stopped him. "My brother axed you a question."

Mac looked down at the hand on his chest. "Asked."

"Yeah. So answer it."

Mac slowly removed Bob's hand. "Don't touch me again. I've got to go. Don't get in my way."

Mac turned right to walk back toward the market and his car, and Doug swung a left-handed haymaker with a trajectory toward Mac's face. He swung his left arm up and turned his head to the right. That blocked the punch and kept it from smashing his nose into a pulp, but the momentum of the fist hitting Mac's forearm into the side of his face snapped his head onto his right shoulder and spiralled him down the drainage ditch.

"What the fuck are you doing around here? What are you looking for?" asked Bob.

Mac looked up from the ditch. "My dog. You guys fucking deaf *and* stupid?" He pushed himself up to a sitting position and held out a hand. "A help up?"

Bob and Doug looked down at him, at each other, and then started laughing.

"Well, I'm glad you're in a better mood." He grabbed a low-hanging branch and pulled himself up. "But your manners are horrible." He brushed debris off his clothes and nodded at them. "Now, as I was saying, I've got to go and—"

Doug drove a fist into Mac's gut and doubled him over. Then, he grabbed him by the head and lifted a knee into Mac's face. Mac got his hands in front of the knee in time to push it away and lashed out with a sharp punch to Doug's groin.

Then Mac straightened fast, catching Doug's rapidly dropping face with the back of his head, stunning him. He lashed out blindly, connecting with something before both arms were pinned behind his back. He struggled against the grip, stepping back into it and driving his heel into the ankle behind him. He took advantage of the surprise and twisted into Bob's grip.

He wrenched one hand free and elbowed Bob in the side of the head before stars burst in his own head, and he dropped face-first into the ditch.

Mac groaned and opened his eyes, then immediately winced. He was headfirst down in the ditch. He took a breath and cried out in pain. "Ah, son of a bitch." He tried pushing himself up, and his left arm collapsed under the pain. He slowly manoeuvred so he wasn't head down, favouring his arm in the process. He sat up, facing away from the road with his back toward the house across the street. He took a few steadying deep breaths. "Son. Of. A. Bitch." He looked up at the sky, then dug his phone out of his pocket. It was awkward because the phone was in his left front pocket, and his left arm was effectively useless.

He finally dug it out with his right hand and looked at the display. Close to 4:00 in the afternoon. He'd been out for over an hour. There was a throbbing pain in the back of his head. He dropped the phone in his lap, reached back and touched the base of his skull. Drew a sharp breath as he touched a sticky wet spot in his hair. "Fuck."

He pulled his hand back and looked at the blood on his fingertips. "Fuck, fuck, fuck." He wiped his hand on his pants, transferring his blood to streaks down his leg. He scrolled through his recent calls list until he found Dawkins' number, then paused. He pocketed the phone without calling and dragged himself to his feet. His head swam. His vision blurred. He looked across the road at the house and tried very hard to pull it into focus. Unsuccessfully. "Fuck."

He sniffed, slid his left arm in through the neck of his polo shirt and walked back to his car, staggering like he'd had three too many at the local pub.

His keys were also in his left-hand pocket. Mac closed his eyes and sighed. "Fuck." He worked the keys out, grunting throughout the exercise. He held them in front of his face, exhausted. Squinted and flipped through them until he found the key to the car door. Three stabs to get it in. Another couple to get the ignition key sorted and in the steering column. "Fuuuuck."

He reached across his body to put the car in Reverse and slowly backed out of the parking spot. He reached across again and put the car in Drive and pointed his car toward the nearest hospital.

Chapter Seventeen

Mac's vision swam as he walked into the A&E entrance of the Wyong hospital. There were half a dozen people waiting in the uncomfortable plastic chairs. A couple of young guys looked like they had been in a fight. A young couple with an abnormally quiet baby. A sturdy-looking guy, a little younger than Mac, was sitting back in his chair, scrolling through something on his phone.

Mac leaned his plastered forehead against the Perspex at the triage nurse's station. He tapped on it with his right index finger. "Help a guy out here?"

The nurse, a young man with "Jason" on his name tag, looked up from paperwork and slid him a clipboard. "Medicare card, please."

Mac groaned, took the clipboard, and placed it on the counter. He struggled to fish his wallet out of his back left pocket with his right hand, then slid the card to the nurse.

Jason entered the Medicare number and looked at the screen. "Malcolm Durridge?"

"As charged."

"Still at this address?"

"Still there. This going to be long?"

Jason slid the card back and looked closer at Mac. "What brings you here?"

Mac held up his left arm. "Something's broken here, and I've got cracked or broken ribs on the same side."

"Accident?"

"Sure as fuck didn't do it on purpose." Mac closed his eyes and took a deep breath, wincing at the pain in his ribs. "Sorry. Had a bit of a disagreement with a couple of blokes. They won."

Jason looked past Mac. "No police? How'd you get here?"

"No cops. Don't need cops. I drove myself. Parking is only free for three hours out there, then it's a ticket. $100 or more. Any chance I'll be out of here before then?"

"Yeah, we'll get you to x-ray right away. Fill in the basics on the clipboard and get it back to me." He picked up the phone and dialled a number as the door behind him opened, and Mac's night got measurably worse.

"Jane," said Mac. "My lucky day."

His ex-wife smiled, which didn't help. She was still a fit 40s, short dark hair, chocolate brown eyes and a permanent smile. Legs that reached all the way to her hips. Some days, he wondered why they split up. Other days, not so much.

"Doctor Jane to you, Mac. You look like shit. What happened?"

"Nothing for you to worry about. Jason is taking care of me."

"I'm sure he is. My shift is over anyway, so you're out of luck."

She smiled at someone behind Mac and walked past him. Mac took the clipboard and followed her as she walked to the sturdy guy who put his phone away, stood, and gave Jane a hug and a kiss.

"Who's this?" asked Mac.

Jane disengaged from the man and turned to face Mac. "Not that it's any of your business at all, but Mac, this is Mark. Mark, Mac used to be married to me. He's not any more. He also used to be a cop, but don't let him intimidate you. It's all bark and no bite."

Mac eased himself into a chair and started filling out the forms. "Nice to meet you, Mark," he said without looking up. "The very best of luck in your relationship with Jane. You're going to need every bit of it. Keep a separate bank account."

Jane snorted, took Mark's hand and walked out. Mac watched them leave, then finished filling out the forms.

Chapter Eighteen

Mac left the hospital into the dark night. A plaster cast weighed down his left arm. The wrist was broken, and the ulna fractured. Four to six weeks in the cast, more than likely six at his age. Or so the doc said. No fractured skull—just a mild concussion—and the ribs were only bruised.

Coordination in the car was no better, but the pain management had improved. He tried moving the car into reverse with his left arm, but the cast restricted his range of motion, and the pressure pushed the pain past the opiate barrier. So it was across-the-body shifting with his right hand. Four to six weeks, the doctor said. "Fuck."

A traffic circle just north of the hospital gave Mac the choice of heading straight through and going home or taking the first exit left and making his way back to the scene of the flogging.

Left it was.

He parked at the same parking lot, in front of the same, now closed, mini-mart. Turned off the ignition and sat in the car, the engine ticking as it cooled the only sound in the overcast night. He took a deep breath and winced as his ribs expanded. "Fuck."

He got out, zippered his jacket against the evening chill and started the walk to the house. A little more circumspect this time. He flipped the hood up on his jacket, slid his hands in his pockets and slowly walked—only the fingertips of the left hand. The cast, old-style plaster, was too large for pockets.

A retirement village was spread out to his right, about halfway to the house. Individual cabins, some lit brighter than others, but all housing locals in the latter stages of their lives in a nice, tidy little community. He envied them. Their lives were sorted—a nice little place, warm, friends living around you.

A blast of cold wind lifted the edges of his hood. He snatched at it with his bad arm, groaning as he grabbed it.

He rounded the corner to the length of road the house sat on. There was one street light between him and it, and it was closer to him than the house. He took a deep breath and walked through the light from the pole and then into the darkness. He stopped in front of the house and slowed his breathing. He slid the hood off his head and listened. About 300 metres behind him, on the other side of the bush, he could hear the faint noise of trucks trundling down the M1. Traffic noise aside, it was quiet. And dark. The house looked cold.

The rail tie he had thrown across the drive was moved to one side. He avoided the gravel drive and walked across the grass to the front stairs. Slow steps up on the edge of the tread, avoiding creaky boards. He placed his hand on the front door, closed his eyes, and listened and felt for any movement in the house.

He stood there for a couple of minutes. Mac looked at his phone. It wasn't that late. If there were anyone in the house, they'd be moving around. He stepped off the porch with less caution and walked to the back of the house. He turned on the light on his phone and checked the back door. The house was supposed to be vacant. It was unlikely the recent occupants would lock the door behind him.

He looked closely at the door jamb and pushed the door open. The wood was splintered around where the deadbolt should be. No locking up in the foreseeable future.

The interior was almost as cold as outside. "Fuck. They must have left right after they cold-cocked me." He flicked on the lights and looked around. It was vacant. Messy, but vacant.

He took a closer look at the house. One of the bedrooms had been occupied more than the others. But there had been more than one person. Obviously. He checked the door. It wasn't secured in any way. He frowned and walked into the lounge area—a small open space beside the kitchen. Paper towels and food remnants were scattered beside a cheap sofa. The kitchen wasn't much better.

He called Kaye. "Hey, Mac here. That last house you showed me? Needs a new lock on the back door."

"Jesus. Thanks for letting me know. That girl was in there?"

Mac looked at the pile of takeout food containers on the kitchen counter. "Maybe. Someone was. I'm going to poke around and look at things, okay with you?"

"Go ahead. I've got to see if I can find someone to secure the door for me." She paused. "Bit of a shit hole inside, isn't it? Does it look like any of the furniture is missing?"

Mac walked back to the bedrooms. "I've seen worse. It looks like you might want to get a cleaner in here, too." He looked in the bedrooms. "Beds are still here. It's hard to say if anything is missing, Kaye. I've never been in here before."

"True. Thanks, Mac. Appreciate the call. Have you got the other list?"

"I don't suppose I have since I have no idea what you're talking about."

"I stopped by your place an hour or so ago and left a list with that young guy you have working for you. A few more possibilities."

"I've been a bit busy. I haven't been back in hours. Thanks. I'll have a look at it when I get home."

He turned off the lights and went out the back door. To keep it shut, he jammed a piece of the splintered wood between the door and the jamb above where it was broken.

He walked back out to the street and stopped, his back to the house. He looked up and down the street. "Back to square one. Where the fuck did you go, Cheryl?"

Mac closed the door to his office apartment, struggled to remove his hoodie over the cast and turned on the heat. He poured a healthy glass of scotch and sat at his desk. Cameron had left Kaye's list of potential bolt holes by the keyboard.

He leaned back in his chair. "What a long, fucking day." He picked up the list and scanned it. The old ones he'd already looked at. He picked up a pen and scratched out the seventh on the list. He'd just been there. Three left. But not tonight.

Tony McFadden

Chapter Nineteen

Mac's headache topped all other headaches he'd ever had. He suspected the concussion diagnosis was correct, but self-employment didn't offer sick days—or vacation days, for that matter.

He closed his eyes and sat back in his chair at his desk. Took a deep breath and slowly stood and wandered into the bathroom. He rustled through drawers until he found the box of generic ibuprofen and codeine. He dry swallowed two and headed back to his desk. There were residual twinges of pain rippling down his left arm, too. He scratched the back of his head with his right hand and yelled. "Fucking fuck. I forgot about that." He gently pressed the plaster back into place on the back of his head. "Explains the headache."

He picked up the list of properties from his desk, carried it to the kitchen, and turned on the kettle. There were three left to look at, all within a fifteen-minute drive.

He scrolled through his contacts and called Dawkins.

"Hey, Dawkins. You got my money?"

"Who is this?"

Mac smiled. "Durridge. Central Coast. I've found her."

There was a pause, and then Mac heard Dawkins' sharp intake of breath. "Where is she?"

"You head up here and call me when you get here. Does she have family? You should notify her family. They're probably worrying about her."

"You let us worry about that. Stay on this number. And stay clear of the location. I'll call you as soon as I get there. Expect me in, oh, about ninety minutes."

Dawkins hung up. Mac looked at his phone and shrugged. "Plenty of time." He picked another number and called. "Cam, lad. I need you to do something for me."

"It's Sunday, Mac."

"Double pay. I want you to do some simple search for me. Find out who Watson's family is. I need to contact them."

"But it's Sunday, Mac."

"I told you. Double pay."

"I told you, Mac. I've got this job. Sweetest AV set-up you've ever seen. Getting introduced to the equipment today, prepping for the big thing later this week."

"Congrats, kid. What time do you have to be there?" Mac eased a jacket sleeve over his cast, tucked the phone between his ear and shoulder and finished putting it on.

"2:00 for a 3:00 start."

"It's only 11:00. Not even. This won't take you more than a couple of minutes, I think. A couple of bills, Cam. Come on."

"Sorry, Mac. No can do. Maybe next time."

"Yeah, great. Good luck. Let me know how it goes. You're a good kid." Mac grabbed the list off the desk, three addresses still not crossed out, and left to finish the search before his client arrived.

The first house was cold and vacant. Right beside it lived a retired couple who spent the better part of their waking hours watching their neighbours. It was not a good stash house.

The second house was different. It sat in a corner of its lot, with ample space between it and the neighbouring houses. Mac pulled to the curb across the street and sat in his car for a minute, watching. A sheer curtain moved slightly in a side window. He flexed his left fist and felt the pain ripple up under the cast—payback time.

He got out of the car and popped the boot. Grabbed a length of pipe and walked across the road and up the driveway. He stopped by the side of the house and listened. The house was quiet, but it didn't feel empty. Mac wasn't sure exactly what it was, but over thirty years of experience in and out of uniform let him know when a place was empty. This one wasn't.

The back door was closed. He slowly turned the knob with his left hand, pipe in his right. He grimaced through the pain. When the latch cleared the door jamb, he flung the door open and rushed in with the pipe high above his head. Someone was sitting at the table in the kitchen, their back to him. He instinctively swung at their back and just managed to check it when his brain registered who it was. The pipe slammed into the tabletop beside her.

Emma spun in her seat with a shriek. "What the fuck?"

"Damn." Mac staggered through the follow-through. "I thought you were someone else."

"I clearly am, you fucking maniac. What the hell?" She saw his cast. "What happened to you?"

"Long story. I'll live. What are you doing here? The Sue and Gerry thing didn't work out?"

She put her head on the table, resting it on her crossed arms. Her voice was muffled. "I don't belong there. I'm the odd one out. They don't want me there."

"Well, you can't stay here. It's someone else's house." Mac tossed the pipe on the table. "There are agencies to help people in your situation."

"Fuck you. You know nothing at all about me."

"Big-assed chip on your shoulder. I want to help. Gerry and Sue want to help." Mac looked around. "Pick up your stuff and come with me. I've got one more house to check out. I'll talk to Ger and Sue after that. They are really good people who really want to help." He sat at the table across from her. "Look, I know you got a shit deal. And that your parents fucked you up. And that all people are shit." He sucked air in through his teeth. "But all people aren't."

"Like I'd go with you. Creep."

Mac shook his head and shrugged. "Look, I can't make you do anything. Truth be told, I don't really *want* to make you do anything." He thought for a second. "You're good with computers, right? All kids are good with computers."

"I don't know what that means. I don't write code."

"I need you to use Google-fu for me. My regular guy has a previous commitment and bailed on me. I'll pay you the same as I paid him. A hundred an hour."

"What is it you really want, Mac?"

"I really want to do the job I was hired to do. I get that you've been fucked around in your very short life, but I'm not that." He paused, looking at a scared fourteen-year-old hiding behind bravado and defiance. "I'm right across from The Pelican. If you don't want to be my geek for this case, you can piss off to The Pelican and hang out there."

Emma scratched at her chin. Seemed to be weighing different options, then stood. "Okay." She stuck out her hand. "Pay in advance."

Mac checked the time on his phone and dug cash out of his pocket. "Five hours worth." He counted the money into her outstretched palm. "Okay?"

"Show me to your computer and tell me what you want to do."

"Let's go." Mac walked out the back door and checked the next address on his list. In Wyong. Fairly large lot. Probably the place. Not far from his place. His phone rang as he got in his car. "Mac speaking."

"Durridge, it's Dawkins. We're in Niagara Park. About thirty minutes out with this traffic. Where are we meeting?"

Mac looked at the paper in his hand and Emma getting into the passenger seat. He cleared his throat. "Pretty sure she's in Wyong. Stopping by there now."

"Pretty sure? I drive up here for pretty sure?"

"Pretty damned sure. It's a small area. Not that many people. Fewer places to hide. She's there. I'll meet you on the street across from the train station." Mac hung up the phone. "Arsehole."

"The case?"

"The case."

Mac stopped at the kerb and motioned for Emma to follow him. She got ahead of him and ran up the steps, two at a time.

"Youth," said Mac.

"Wasted on the young, I hear." She stood by the door, waiting for him. Bolted in when he unlocked the door, sat at his desk and wiggled the mouse. The screen lit up asking for password.

"I'll enter it."

"You're going to have to give it to me. If it locks while you're out, you don't want me calling you, right?"

Mac grunted and wrote his password on a sticky note. "Try finding Cheryl Watson's family. Mother, father, any siblings. I don't know anything about them. They'll need to be contacted."

"Why?"

"Why what?"

"Why will they need to be contacted?"

"They will. See what you can find." He tapped on his desk. "I've got to run. Send me what you've got when you get it."

"Your mobile number?"

Mac picked up her phone and sent himself a text. He returned the phone to her and stored the number in his phone to contacts.

Emma nodded. "Right. Got it."

Chapter Twenty

Mac pulled to the curb across the street from the last house on the list. Big corner lot, backing on bush. He turned off the ignition and settled in his seat. He had the right place. The car was parked in the back, the rear quarter panel extending past the side of the house. This was easy money. He looked at his watch. Fifteen minutes until Dawkins arrived. As he figured it, the guy would be arriving with an army to take out the kidnappers, somehow, and finish this once and for all.

And maybe drop another large bag of cash at his feet.

He settled into his seat, an eye on the Statesman. I wouldn't do it if they took off with their victim before Dawkins and his boys arrived. Probably *no* more bags of cash if that happened.

He clenched his left fist against the pain. Looked at the house and contemplated exacting some revenge. He then reconsidered. The money would be revenge enough.

His phone rang. He looked at the display and saw it coming from his office. "Emma? You've got something for me?" He slid down in his seat a bit. "Found some family?"

"I did some digging. Hers is a pretty private family. I can't find any parents."

"Shit. Well, you tried."

"You should let me finish, Mac. I did find someone."

One of the two apes who broke his arm stepped out of the front door, looked straight at Mac in his car, and returned to the house. Mac sat up and cursed. "Emma, I've got to go. Things are happening."

"She's got two brothers."

"Where do they live?"

"Country NSW. Want me to send you the info?"

"Yes. Please. Thanks. Treat yourself. Tell The Pelican I'll pay for whatever you want."

Mac hung up, and a chime from his phone indicated an incoming message. He opened a photo of Cheryl and four men tagged with an address in Orange. He recognised the photo. Cam had sent him the same one. Emma had tagged two of the men. He tapped on the photo and zoomed in on their faces. The two men who had beat the shit out of him. Tagged with the names Bob and Doug. "Fuck."

He looked at the time and swore. Scrolled through the numbers on his phone and called Dawkins. "Hey, mate, meet me at the *Wyoming* Station, right? We can travel together from there."

"Wyoming? You said Wyong."

"No. Why in the fuck would I say Wyong? I'm in Wyoming. Just a bit north of Gosford. How long will you be? I thought you'd be here by now. This is moving fast."

"You said Wyong."

"Fuck, Dawkins, I don't have time for this kind of shit. Wyoming. As fast as you can get here." Mac hung up. He looked at his new phone and sighed. "Son of a bitch." He rubbed his face, got out of the car and dropped the phone on the pavement. He shook his head and drove his heel into the screen, shattering it. He stomped on it a couple of more times, then headed for the house.

Dawkins looked at his phone. "Fucking hell."

"What's wrong, boss?"

"How far away are we from Wyoming?"

Wilson entered some data in his GPS and looked at Dawkins. "Thirty minutes. Why?"

"That fucking PI just lied to me. Said he told me he was in Wyoming when I know for a fucking fact he said Wyong." He punched a number into his phone. "He must think I'm some kind of fucking moron." He waited for someone to answer his call. "Matthias, Dawkins here. I need a location. I'll text you the number. And I need it in five minutes. General location is good enough. Either Wyong or

Wyoming. Text me when you know." He terminated the call and sent Mac's number to his contact.

Bob looked out the window at the man approaching the house. "We need to get the fuck out of here. That arsehole from yesterday is outside."

Doug pushed him to one side and looked through the venetian blind slats. "The punk. I'll take care of him."

Bob grabbed his brother by the arm. "Not worth the attention. We need to grab Cheryl and get out of here."

Doug pulled his arm free and opened the front door as Mac walked up the steps. "Moot point, bro. He wants to mix it up."

Dawkins leaned an elbow out the passenger's window and his chin on his hand. His phone beeped, and he lifted his head. An address was displayed on his phone screen. "Wyong. The fucking dick." He slapped Wilson on the arm and showed him the address on his phone. "There. Step on it."

Mac raised a hand to knock, and the door was flung open. The guy who threw the punch that knocked him out was in front of him, fist cocked and ready to deliver the blow.

"Hang on, pal. Doug, right? Hang on. We got off on the wrong foot before. Give me thirty seconds. If I haven't convinced you, hit me all you want."

Doug frowned and took a half step back. "Who the fuck are you, and why the fuck are you tracking me down?"

"My name's Mac Durridge. Your sister's husband hired me to track her down. Told me that she was kidnapped. Promised me the ransom money if I tracked her down and took out the kidnappers." Mac held up his hands as Doug advanced. "I know, I know. That's bullshit. Unfortunately, there's a team of heavies a couple of minutes behind me who aren't as nice as I am. You need to get the hell out of here."

Bob pulled in beside Doug. "Bullshit."

"No, I believe him," said Doug.

Mac strained to look over the shoulders of the two brothers and saw Cheryl. She looked better than in the picture but more frazzled. She pushed her brothers aside and stood face-to-face with Mac. "How much time?"

"Less than five minutes."

"Is Dawkins working this for him?"

Mac nodded. "Yeah. Glad you're okay. Why are you running from your husband?"

"I don't have time right now, Mac. We need to get the hell out of here. Don't follow us." She stepped back into the house and slammed the door in his face.

Mac took a reflexive step back. He patted his pockets and remembered where his phone was. "Shit." He stepped off the front step and had to jump out of the way as the car screamed out of the drive. He trotted across the road to what was left of his mobile phone and picked through the debris until he found his SIM card. He slid it in his pocket and got in his car. He pulled away from the curb and headed in the direction Cheryl and her brothers went. He glanced in his rear-view mirror as he rounded the corner at the end of the block. A black SUV was coasting to a stop in front of where he smashed his phone.

Chapter Twenty-One

Mac smacked his steering wheel in frustration. He eased around the corner and pulled to the curb. Jumped out of his car, pulled the hood up on his jacket and walked back to the corner. He leaned against a tree.

Dawkins' SUV had already stopped near where Mac had dropped his phone, and two other trucks had pulled in behind him. The doors opened, and six very large men exited. They huddled around Dawkins for a moment, then split off in pairs, going house to house. Mac watched for a minute, then returned to his car.

It took Mac fifteen minutes to get back to his office. He took the stairs two at a time and stopped halfway up the thirty-seven steps. "Shit." He ran back down and down the street to the service station. Grabbed a prepay SIM card and tossed a twenty on the counter. "Keep the change, Jenny."

He ran back up the stairs and entered his apartment, winded. Emma had left. A note by his keyboard told him she was across the street at The Pelican.

He rifled through his desk drawers until he found an old iPhone. A previous generation. He straightened out a paperclip, popped out the SIM tray and inserted the prepay SIM. He plugged the phone into his computer and synched to a previous backup. The battery was at 7%. He sat back and laced his fingers behind his head. Put his feet up on the desk. Closed his eyes. He needed to think through options.

Dawkins clenched his jaw muscles and knocked on a storm door. He looked to his left at one of his guys doing the same thing two houses down. He took a step back and stood, feet shoulder width, hands crossed in front of his groin, phone in one hand. He waited while footsteps inside the house got louder.

The interior door opened a couple of inches and an eyeball peered around it. "Who are you and what do you want?"

"Lawrence Dawkins. I'm an investigator looking for a missing woman." He held up his phone with a picture of Cheryl. "Have you seen her around here recently?"

The door opened wider, and a middle-aged woman in a threadbare bathrobe stepped closer to the storm door. She squinted and peered at the photo on the phone. "Isn't that the Prime Minister's wife?" she snapped her fingers. "Sherry? No, Cheryl. Right?"

Dawkins took the phone away and slid it into his breast pocket. "No, I think you're mistaken. There is a slight similarity, true, but this woman, the woman I'm looking for, isn't named Cheryl. It's Shannon. She's missing and has a medical condition that needs fairly immediate attention. Have you seen her, or someone who looks like her in the neighbourhood?"

The woman looked at Dawkins for a minute, then shook her head. "Nope. Nobody looking like that. Sorry." She stepped back and swung the door closed. The snick of the bolt sliding into place punctuated her action.

"Fucking hell." He stepped off the front step and walked to the next house when his phone rang. The number was blocked. "Who is this?"

"Where the fuck are you, Dawkins?"

"Durridge? Where the fuck are *you*?" Dawkins stood in the middle of the road and circled his hand above his head, rounding up his squad.

"Wyoming. Like I said. You should have been here by now. I'm parked across the street from the train station. You better hurry up. I think they're getting ready to run with her."

"Bullshit, Durridge. What fucking game are you playing? *You're* not in Wyoming, and *she's* not in Wyoming. Where are you hiding her?" Dawkins held his hand up as his men gathered around him on the street. Put his fingers to his lips.

"What are you talking about? Hiding her? Where are you? Jesus, Dawkins, You better not be in Wyong. You'll never get here in time. Shit. I've got to go. They're leaving. Hurry the fuck up."

The call dropped. Dawkins looked at his phone and shook his head. "What a load of shit." He dialled a number and waited for an answer. "Matthias. I need you to find the number that just called me. Get me the number and a location. And fucking fast." He hung up and looked at his men. "Keep looking. She's around here somewhere."

Mac hung up and gently placed the phone on his desk. "That might buy me an hour. Maybe." He checked the battery. 63%. He unplugged the phone, grabbed a couple of paperclips and headed back to the service station.

Jenny looked up from a movie magazine as he entered. She pulled a five-dollar bill from the till. "Your change, Mac."

He waved her away. Grabbed a fistful of prepay SIM packets from a hanging rack and dropped them on the counter. "All of these."

Jenny spread them out and counted. "Why do you need six cards?" She held up her hand. "Never mind. Plausible deniability. You find that klepto yet?"

She scanned each of them individually and rang up the total.

"Still looking." Mac pulled a fold of bills from his pocket. "How much?"

"One twenty. Unlimited local calls and text, and 2GB of data. Expires in a month if you don't top it up."

"I'm only going to need them for a couple of days, I think."

Jenny nodded and butted the edges of the SIM packets together and pushed the stack toward him. "Happy calling."

Dawkins stepped off yet another porch and stood in the middle of the road. He slowly turned in a circle. The houses were low-end, mostly single-story, single-car driveways. Most actually didn't have a garage, just a carport. The landscaping was non-existent. "This place is a shit hole. What was she doing here?"

One of his men ran up the road to him. "Boss, we found it, I think." He pointed down the road to a puke green house with a rusty awning over the front door and a car port that looked like it was leaning into the wind. "Evidence that someone was there and has left recently, and fast."

Dawkins trotted up the street behind the man and followed him into the house. "Show me."

"Takeout food bags. This kebab is still warm. The beer is cold. There are no furnishings. Makes sense this was the place."

Dawkins pushed the kebab to one side and frowned. His phone chimed with an incoming message, and he looked at the screen. A phone number and a location. He dialled the number.

Mac answered. "Is that you, Dawkins?"

"You're not in Wyoming, Mac. And I'm in the house they were in before you took them. Where did you take them?"

"I'm confused, Dawkins. I thought this was a kidnapping."

Dawkins squeezed the phone and pressed it harder to the side of his head. "You're fucking with things you have no idea about. And if you think you can hide her from me, you're sadly mistaken."

The call terminated. Mac looked at his phone, sighed, and turned it off. He dug a paperclip from one pocket and a cardboard packet with a new SIM card from another. He slid out the compromised SIM and installed the new one. He double-checked the settings on the phone and made sure his caller ID wasn't displayed on outgoing calls. It was still set for 'blocked call'. "Interesting."

Chapter Twenty-Two

Cheryl peered out the back window as Doug drove. After the third corner, with nobody following, she turned in her seat and tapped Bob on the shoulder. "Who in the hell was that guy?" She took a quick glance over her shoulder. "Do you believe him?"

Bob turned in his seat. "That he's working for your husband? Yes." He licked his lips. "That he's actually now trying to help us? Hell no."

"How did he find us so fast?" asked Cheryl.

"Doug and I haven't turned our phones on in two days. It wasn't us. What about you? Have you turned it on?"

"The last time my phone was on, I was talking to my husband," she spat out that word, "two days ago. You know what's happened since then." Cheryl looked past her brother and out the windscreen. "Where to now?"

They drove in silence, threading through traffic in Morisset. Then Doug grunted and pulled a hard right across traffic.

Cheryl slammed against the door. "What the hell, bro?"

"Debbie's place. Her parent's place."

Cheryl shook her head. "They live in Wollongong. "

"No, sis, their summer place. That caravan park near Budgie. It'll be empty."

Cheryl chewed the inside of her cheek and thought for a minute. "Not bad. George doesn't know about her." She half smiled and looked at her brother. "What made you think about Deb? It's been years."

"The one that got away. Sit back and look bored. We don't want to attract attention."

Chapter Twenty-Three

He was back to square one. Cheryl was in the wind, and Mac had no idea where to start. And he was starving.

He crossed to The Pelican and flagged down Jessie. "Hey, I need something quick." He looked around. "Did Emma come over here?"

"She's in a booth at the back with a pizza and some cola," said Jessie. "Quick, like what?"

"Quick, like whatever fast food is cooked, I'll take it. I'm starving and need to be somewhere."

Jessie stood on her tip-toes and looked over the counter into the kitchen. "Onion rings. I could get someone to whip up a burger if you've got five minutes."

"Very kind, but I'm in a real bind. All the onion rings. That'll have to do. How much?"

"My treat." While Jessie walked around to the kitchen, Mac walked to the back of the restaurant to look for Emma. She was sitting at a booth in the far corner, finishing off a pepperoni pizza.

"Hey, Mac. All good?"

"I was about to ask the same thing. Settled?"

She shrugged. "I guess. I'm helping out in the kitchen after I finish eating. So I'm in no hurry to finish eating."

"So you're going to hang around this time?"

Emma chewed on the last of the crust. "We'll see. Did you find the woman yet?"

"No, and I've got to get going. Stay good."

Mac walked down the sidewalk from The Pelican to Nazmi's kebab shop, eating onion rings from his takeaway bag. A throng of mostly drunk footy fans were buying slices of pizza and kebabs, spilling out onto the street. He lingered on the sidewalk until the shop was clear and poked his head in. "Habib, I need you to keep an eye out for me, okay?"

"Sure thing, Mac," said Nazmi. "For what?"

Mac opened the photos on his phone and scrolled to the shot of Cheryl and her two brothers. "One of these apes might be by picking up some food. Let me know if either of them shows up."

Nazmi stood a little straighter and crossed his arms, flexing his considerable biceps. "You want me to detain them for you?"

Mac laughed. "Oh, hell no. They're good guys. I just need to find them." He held out his hand. "Give me your phone." He took it and sent himself a text message. "Let me know, okay?"

Nazmi took his phone back. "No problem, Mac." He held up his phone. "I already had your number."

"Not this one. Thanks."

Dawkins slammed his fist repeatedly onto the steering wheel. Pressed his phone hard to his head. "I said fucking find him, Matthias. You know the number. Track him."

"It's been offline for over an hour now. If it shows up, I'll call you."

"He's probably switched numbers again."

"I'll see what I can do."

Dawkins growled. "Do it faster." He stabbed the disconnect button and threw the phone on the dashboard. "Fucking hell." He looked at his right-hand man. "Spread out. There aren't many places around here. Two head down to Gosford; the rest pair up and start door-knocking. People around here know that Durridge fuck. Tell them we're looking for him because he's come into money or something. Check in every piss-ant town from here to Hornsby." He took a deep breath. "Fucking find him!"

Mac scrolled through his contacts and found who he was looking for. "Kaye, I need some help."

"You can't afford to buy, Mac. So you must still be looking for hiding places."

Mac leaned against the back wall of The Pelican. "I've hit all the vacation homes. Do you know of any other vacancies where some people might be keeping their heads down?"

"I don't think—hang on a second."

Mac listened to the clicking of a keyboard for a few seconds. "What do ya got, Kaye? I'm in a bit of a rush."

The clacking stopped and Mac listened to silence. "You're making some assumptions that I don't necessarily agree with," said Kaye.

"Probably. I apologise if I sound a little short. Lives hang in the balance."

Kaye laughed. "Sure. Look, any other vacancies around here, I've visited in the past twenty-four hours. They're empty and locked up."

"Shit." Mac pressed the phone against his head and looked around, thinking.

"Who is hiding from you? Who are you looking for?"

"Confidential case stuff, Kaye. Thanks for your help. I appreciate it."

"No problem."

Mac terminated the call, slid the phone in his pocket and walked out of the alley and into the main street. Turned left and spotted two of Dawkins' men. Two of the big ones. One was showing a photo on his phone to a passer-by who was pointing across the street to Mac's apartment. He slipped back into the alley. "Son of a bitch."

The phone in his pocket vibrated, and he walked further into the alley and answered it. "Who's this?"

"Kaye."

"How'd you get this number, Kaye?"

"You just called me, Mac. Your phone number came up on my screen."

"Shit."

"Right. Anyway, I had a thought."

Mac looked over his shoulder and stepped into the shadows. "About what?"

"You've checked the vacation homes and the vacancies are all accounted for, right?"

"We just talked about that," said Mac. "What's your point?"

"Caravan parks." Kaye paused. "Caravan parks. Get it?"

"Not really."

"It's winter. Most of the caravans are vacant. They tend to be summer places. Some of them are occupied year-round, but the majority are empty at this time of year. And there's a big park not far from Budgie. I think it holds sixty caravans."

Mac smiled. "You've been extremely helpful, Kaye. I owe you dinner. When this is done, I'll treat you. Your choice."

"I look forward to it. Let me know if you need anything else."

Mac hung up and checked the settings on his phone. He switched the anonymous call feature on. "Fuck. How did I miss that?"

He walked to the end of the alley and peered around the corner. The two gorillas were easing quietly up the stairs to his office, hands under their jackets. "Great." He looked at his car in the parking lot behind his apartment building. "It's going to be a long night."

He returned to the back of The Pelican and knocked on the kitchen door. After a minute, Sue opened the door and nodded him in.

"Thanks, Sue."

"Some apes are looking for you. What did you do?"

"Long story. Mind if I hang out in your kitchen? They're going through my apartment right now. Rather not have to face off against them."

"Come on in. I'll get you some food."

Chapter Twenty-Four

Gerry turned the lights off behind the bar and walked into the kitchen. Mac was leaning back in a chair, eyes half closed.

"Mac, I've got to lock up." Gerry looked at his watch. "It's past 1:00. You need to split."

"I will. Thanks for the bolt hole. How's Emma doing?"

"Sue's in full mother-hen mode. I think she'll be okay. Out like a light in the guest room." He looked at his watch again.

Mac yawned and stretched and stood. "Yeah, yeah. Thanks. I'll go out the back."

"Sure. Let me know if you need anything, okay?" He clapped Mac on the back. "Take it easy."

Mac stepped into the back alley, pulled the collar up on his jacket and shivered. "Always do, Ger. Catch you later. Thanks again."

He walked to the end of the alley and looked around the corner. The stairs to his place beckoned. Lights shone through his windows, though, and he knew he'd turned the lights off when he left. "Well, fuck."

He trotted across the empty street and slowly walked up the metal stairs, minimising the noise from his shoes. The door was partially open, a beam of light slicing across the landing. He stood there for a minute, listening intently. A car started across the street. A dog barked in the distance.

His apartment was still. If there was anyone in there, they were as quiet as he was. He took a deep breath and slammed the door open—the element of surprise.

The door slammed against the inside wall and bounced back. He held his left hand up and stopped the rebound. "Jesus." He put the cast under his right arm and took a deep breath. "Man, that hurt."

The place was empty. But it was a mess. The desk was tipped over, and the lamp and computer were on the floor. The file cabinet drawers were all pulled open, and paper was strewn across the floor. Chairs were overturned. "Fucking hell."

He closed and locked the door. Grabbed one of the chairs and wedged the back under the knob. Gave the door a tug and grunted in satisfaction.

He stepped into the living area behind the office. The mattress was flipped against the wall, and the clothes were off their hangers and strewn across the floor. He grabbed the mattress and flipped it back on the bed frame, positioned it straight, and sat on it. His eyes were heavy, and the bed beckoned, but he needed to take inventory. Old police habits die hard. He sighed and shook his head.

He picked up the scattered furniture and was sliding the file cabinet drawers shut when it hit him.

"Shit." He yanked the bottom drawer open and moved the files away. The cash was gone. He slowly stood. He pulled the thinning wad of cash from his pocket and counted it—a little over three thousand left. Two spent and ninety-five stolen. Stolen by the arsehole who gave it to him

He yawned and walked back to his bedroom. He rubbed his eyes with the heels of his hands and flopped back on the bed. "Tomorrow." He closed his eyes and was asleep in seconds.

Mac woke the next morning and immediately checked the file cabinet. The cash was still gone. "Easy come. Shit."

He checked the time on his phone and swore again. He had to get to Cheryl before anyone else did. He grabbed the car keys and ran down the stairs.

The temperature was in the single digits and the light rain looked like it would get heavy before it ended. The car heater was cranked, forcing hot air up the windscreen in a valiant fight against the condensation.

He pulled into the visitor's parking area of the caravan park Kaye had told him about. He got out of his car and into the shitty weather and flipped up his hood. The gate was closed but not latched. It was a gate designed to stop cars, not people.

Kaye was right. Most of the caravans were empty. The whole park looked desolate. Most of the drives adjacent to the caravans were empty. The park was laid out in four concentric half circles. He walked along the outer ring, peering into front doors or through kitchen windows at the end of the caravans. Most were empty.

One that was clearly occupied was at the end of the first row. The front window was cracked open, and steam billowed out. A small flower garden took the place of the hitch, most of the flowers dead, protected by a low wooden fence. He saw a figure behind the steam and tapped on the window. The woman let out a little shriek, her cigarette dropping out of her mouth, as he peered into what turned out to be the kitchen.

"Sorry, ma'am. I'm looking for a woman and her two brothers. They were supposed to meet me here, but didn't tell me which caravan they were staying in." He held up the group photo on his phone. "Have you seen any of these three people?"

She scrambled to pick up her cigarette and peered through the dirty kitchen window. She looked at the photo, then at Mac, then at the photo and past Mac. She shook her head and stepped back, cranking the louvred window shut and pulling the curtains over her sink closed with a snap of her wrist.

"What the fuck was that?" Mac shook his head and turned and came face-to-face with the larger of Cheryl's two brothers. "Fuck! How's it going, Doug?"

"You're persistent."

Mac looked past him at the other brother. He smiled and held out his hand. "I was hired to find your sister. You're Bob, right? I know that you haven't kidnapped the Prime Minister's wife but are, in fact, protecting her from someone. Those someones are not that far behind me."

"And I'm going to fucking flatten you." Bob ignored Mac's hand and shoved him in the chest. Mac stumbled backward and tripped over the low fencing protecting the garden. He landed on his arse in the dirt and scrambled backwards. Bob approached, both fists clenched.

"Hang on, man. I'm serious. Dawkins and his guys are around here intent on finding you."

Doug ran up behind Bob and grabbed his brother's wrist. "How do you know that name? And how did they manage to get this close?"

Mac slowly stood and brushed dirt off his backside. "He hired me. And I may have led them here. But they misled me." Mac looked around for Cheryl. "Where are you staying?"

"One row in, on the end," said Doug. "We need to get out of sight."

"Fuck off, bro." Bob crossed his arms and stood in front of his brother. "This fuck nut tracked us here. We need to get rid of him."

Doug laughed. "You're sounding like an idiot. Don't be a dick. Come on." He trotted down the road to a medium-sized caravan in a relatively clean state. The black Statesman was parked beside it.

"Who owns this place?" asked Mac. "Dawkins has good resources. He can find anybody."

"Nah," said Doug. "Not this place. No obvious connection. Parents of an old girlfriend, but we've kept in touch. They're in the Kimberly for the next month. The key was where it always was. In one of the hanging potted plants." He opened the door and stood to one side. "Get in. Quickly."

The layout was standard caravan. A small kitchen to the left of the door, and beyond that, a bathroom and a double bed. There was a table to the right that looked like it dropped into a single bed. Cheryl was sitting at the table. Mac gravitated toward her. She was poised and coiled, a study in contained anger. Her short dark hair was offset by piercing blue eyes, bluer than any picture could convey.

He held out his hand. "Cheryl. I'm sorry I've put you in this situation. I was misled by your husband's agents."

She shook his hand. "Vinnie? Ya gotta watch out for Vinnie." She motioned for him to sit across from her. "But don't worry about it. They're only devious, immoral criminals who want to kill me."

Mac slid into the seat across from Cheryl. Her brothers kept watch, Bob looking out the door window and Doug keeping an eye on his little sister. "We need to get you out of here. We aren't safe."

Chapter Twenty-Five

Cheryl laughed. "I haven't been safe for over a year. This is me finally getting off my arse and fighting back. I need to figure out the end game."

"Ya shoulda figured that out before you left," said Bob.

She side-eyed him. "Shut up, Bob. I'm talking."

He crossed his arms and continued to stare out the window.

Cheryl stared at him a minute, then continued. "This probably isn't a surprise to any half-decently intelligent person, but there's an element of corruption in any political position. Some clearly much worse and more obvious than others, but it's there, an undercurrent to everything the politicians do. No different for George. But I rationalised it by balancing it against the good work he did." She sighed and ran her fingers through her hair. "But the higher he moved in political circles, the harder it got to keep that balance. Corners were cut, people hurt, and eventually, it passed the point I was willing to accept it."

"So leave."

She snorted. "If only it were that easy. I haven't been that lily-white myself." She held up a hand. "Not anywhere near as bad as George was, but fraudulent expenses, some legislation that helped the family. Mice nuts compared to what George has elevated himself to over the past couple of years."

"I still don't get it. Corruption is expected. There hasn't been an honest politician in the history of politicians. Why this chase?"

Cheryl dug into her pocket and pulled out a USB drive. "Bank records. Financial transactions. Correspondence with alleged opponents to make backroom deals against the interests of the party and the country. Bribes. Outright, straight up massive bribes."

"So send it to a couple of reporters and hide out for a while."

Bob chuckled wryly. "Like we're stupid or something. Don't you think we'd have thought of that by now?"

"George has the media in his pocket," said Cheryl. "It'd get spiked, and I'd be disappeared." She looked at Mac's surprised face. "Like Sopranos disappeared. Like getting dropped out of a plane over the outback halfway between here and Muswellbrook.

Mac sat and thought for a minute. "Yeah, I'm still not getting it. Look at the shit Trump got away with, and all he had to do was deny it. If Georgie has the media where he wants them, like you say, he wouldn't care about what you had. He wouldn't be chasing you. And he sure as hell wouldn't be hiring me and, I assume, a dozen others to track you down." He scratched his jaw. "You've got something a hell of a lot worse than financial improprieties." He shrugged. "Or you'd have given it to the cops."

Cheryl sighed. "I've been holding this over his head for a couple of weeks. He thought I was joking at first, but three days ago, he tried to kill me." She held up her hands. "Can't prove it was him, but I don't believe in coincidences. You're right. It's not *just* financial improprieties. It's a level of corruption Trump would envy."

Doug moved to the table and sat beside Cheryl. "A dozen others? Fuck. "He looked around. "We're going to have to get the hell out of here."

"And go where?" Cheryl chewed the inside of her cheek. She visibly deflated. "I'm getting tired of running." She lowered her head and rested it on her arms. "I don't know the end game."

"There's stuff about you on that thing, too. Right?"

Cheryl lifted her head and looked at Mac. "Yeah, I've already admitted I'm not completely clean." She reached across the table and tapped Mac on the back of his hand. "So why are you doing this? The money?"

Mac sniffed. "I certainly appreciated the money, but I was 'rescuing' you from a kidnapping. That's how Dawkins presented it to me. And he's a very convincing man."

"And Vinnie, too."

"And Vinnie." Mac paused and shook his head. "And I really hate being made a fool of." He looked at the time on his phone. "It's still early. We need to get that information you have to someone who can get it out into the world." He looked around the caravan. "I don't suppose you've got a laptop here?"

Cheryl laughed. "No connectivity to anything. He can find me if I pop my electronic head up. And I don't know where to go from here. He won't stop until I'm dead."

Doug crossed his arms. "Fuck that."

Bob looked out the window at the front of the caravan, over the kitchen sink. "Hold that thought." Bob adjusted his stance and motioned Mac over. "Do you recognise these guys?"

Mac looked at the two muscle-heads coming up the road toward the trailer. "Yeah. Is there a back way out of here?"

"It's a caravan. There's only one way out. But not to worry. There are only two of them. We can take them," said Doug. He pushed open the door and stepped onto the road. Bob scrambled after him.

Mac shook his head. "Big mistake." He held out his hand, palm outward toward Cheryl. "Stay here. It's going to get ugly."

"I still don't know who you are, so I'll pretend that you didn't say that. Get out of my way." Cheryl pushed past him and walked out behind her brothers.

"Oh, shit." Mac took a deep breath and joined the party outside. Doug was already engaged.

"Who sent you?" asked Doug. The two men, both slightly shorter than Doug but broader in the shoulders, didn't slow their pace. They walked side by side, about two metres apart, advancing toward Mac, Bob, Doug and Cheryl.

Bob stepped beside his brother and put his hands out. The two visitors were about ten metres away. "Whoa, guys. Dawkins send you?"

They kept walking, not talking. Cheryl pushed between her brothers and stood slightly in front of them. "Tell Dawkins to tell Vinnie to tell my husband to fuck right off. Got it? He's not going to get what he's looking for. And if he leaves me alone, it'll never come to light."

Doug took his sister by the shoulders and moved her to one side. "I think she told you to fuck off, mates."

The man on the right finished typing something on his phone and slid it into his inside suit pocket. His hand came out with a knife. His friend pulled one out also and lunged at Doug, slicing at his torso. Doug fell to the ground, holding his stomach, blood pulsing through his fingers.

"Doug!" Cheryl's rush forward was stopped by Mac grabbing her wrist. She tried shaking herself free and stumbled, a knife blade singing past her face, just missing her cheek. "Son of a bitch." She swung out with her foot and caught the attacker on the knee as she fell.

Mac stepped in front of her and drove his right elbow into her attacker's jaw. He instinctively followed up with a left and, just in time, pulled his punch, looking at his cast instead of the assailant. He saw the blade at the last second, ducking out of the way and landing on his broken arm. "Jesus fucking Christ." He rolled out of the way and scrambled to his feet.

Doug crawled to the caravan door, a trail of blood marking his path. Bob was on the ground, grappling with the other assailant and not looking like he was gaining an upper hand.

Cheryl grabbed a rock from the planter outside the trailer and swung at the man who stabbed Doug. Mac rolled to his feet, grabbed another rock and hit Bob's attacker on the back of the head twice. He turned and saw the other attacker on top of Cheryl, choking her.

Mac ran over and kneed him in the ribs, then brought the rock down on his head. The attacker rolled and raised his arm, deflecting the blow and swinging a fist up toward Mac's groin. Mac pivoted, caught the punch on the inside of his thigh, and raised his arm to hit him again when Cheryl crowned the guy with her rock.

Mac looked at him for a second, then hobbled over to Doug. "Bob, grab an arm. We need to get off the street." Mac held up one side of Doug while Bob took the other. "Back in the trailer for now. Cheryl, grab their phones."

Chapter Twenty-Six

Bob and Mac placed Doug on the bed. "Cheryl, get some scissors and cut off his shirt. Hold something over the cut. I need to get rid of those two bodies. Bob, give me a hand." He held up his cast. "I'm not a hundred per cent."

Cheryl scrambled through a drawer in the kitchen. "Hang on, Dougie. You'll be good."

Mac glanced at her, then ran back onto the street outside the caravan, with Bob behind him.

"Is he going to be okay?"

"I don't know. It looks serious. Look, we need to immobilise these guys for the duration." The one who stabbed Doug was stirring. Mac took a long step and kicked him in the head. "Drag them into the bushes and make sure they're out for a while." He grabbed a leg and started dragging, backing into the bush surrounding the caravan park. He was struggling to get the guy over a ridge of brick edging the walkway when Bob ran over to help.

"How long will these guys be out?" Bob grabbed the other leg and helped pull.

"Hard to say. An hour or so, I guess. But they'll be shit when they come around. It's not like the movies. Their eggs are going to be scrambled." He gave one more heave and dropped the leg. "This'll do. Let's get back and see how Doug is doing."

Cheryl had Doug's polo shirt cut open, his pale flesh pink with blood. She pressed a tea towel against his side.

"What's it look like, Cheryl?" Bob rested his hand on her shoulder. "How you doing, bro?"

Doug groaned. "Fuck."

Cheryl eased up the towel and exposed a cut along her brother's side. "Not that deep, but bleeding like a son of a bitch. We need to get him to the hospital." She paused. "But we can't."

"I need to call someone." Mac patted his pockets. "Where's the phones you took off the meat heads?"

"On the counter. SIMs removed. Do you think it's a good idea? There's a landline in here somewhere."

Mac skipped the mobiles and found an old phone nailed to the wall. He thought for a second, trying to recall the number. Then he took a deep breath and dialled.

"This is Jane."

"Jane, don't hang up, this is Mac."

"I'm hanging up."

"No, please, don't. Are you working today?"

"Just came off my shift. And one reason why I shouldn't hang up on you?"

Mac took a deep breath, looked at Doug and Cheryl and hoped his explanation would work. "I need your help. It's a long story, but there's a guy with his gut sliced open, and his sister is trying to stem the flow, but we need professional help. You've told me many times that you're the best doctor on the north coast, so I'd like you to make a house call and help me out."

"Take him to the hospital, Mac. Good-bye." Jane hung up.

"Who's Jane?"

Mac looked at Cheryl. "Ex-wife." He pressed re-dial. "We didn't split on good terms."

"Fuck off, Mac," said Jane as she answered.

"No, no, no. Please don't hang up. We can't go to the hospital. Someone is trying to kill us. All of us."

There was a long pause on the line.

"Jane?"

"Call the police, then. And they'll take him to the hospital."

"Come on, Jane. If it was that easy, don't you think I'd have thought of it already?" He closed his eyes and leaned his head against the wall. "Fuck's sake, do you think I'd actually call you if I didn't have to?" He gave her the address of the caravan park. "Lot 34. Do what's right, okay?"

He hung up the phone and slumped against the counter. "Fingers crossed." He joined Cheryl and Bob. "How is he?"

"I'm right here," said Doug. "And I hurt like a son of a bitch. How far away is the Jane chick, and will she have any drugs with her?"

Mac eased up the cloth and looked at the cut. "She lives in Lake Munmorah. Five minutes, max. *If* she comes. The bleeding is slowing down, but it still looks like shit. Who owns this caravan?"

"*If* she comes?" Doug clenched his teeth against the pain. "Don't you know anyone who *will* come?"

"She's the best I know around here. This place is an old girlfriend's parent's place, right?"

"Yeah," said Doug through gritted teeth. "From a long time ago. I don't think anyone from Cheryl's side of the family knows about it. But there's the matter of the two guys in the bush. They'll be able to find them pretty quickly.

"Shit. Right." Mac took a breath. "So oldies live here. So there's probably some peroxide in here somewhere," he said. "That cut needs to be cleaned."

He ducked into the bathroom and came out with a small plastic bottle. He unscrewed the lid and nodded at Cheryl. "Move that cloth out of the way."

She slowly lifted it and stepped to one side. Mac poured a trickle of hydrogen peroxide along the wound, watching it bubble and fizz as it hit the open cut.

Doug tensed. "Fuuuuuck, man. That stings."

"Killing the germs, my mum used to say." Mac screwed the cap back on and took the cloth from Cheryl, folded it over to a clean spot, and pressed it on the wound. "We need to close that hole in your side, somehow, and get the hell out of here."

Bob called from the window. "Mac, what's the Jane Doctor look like?"

"Tall, short dark hair, kinda thin."

"That her?"

Mac looked out the window, then opened the door. "Jane, you walk here?"

Jane walked up the steps, a backpack over her left shoulder. "I parked around the corner. I couldn't find the place. What in the hell is going on?"

"It's a really long story, and we need to get out of here before trouble shows up," said Mac.

Jane dropped her bag on the counter. "Show me why I'm here."

Chapter Twenty-Seven

"I've got pain meds if you need them," said Jane. She turned the water on as hot as it went and scrubbed her hands. "Varying strengths from Ibuprofen to serious stuff that'll knock you out."

Doug looked up at Mac, who shook his head.

"Nothing too strong. We need him mobile," said Mac. "Too big to carry. He's going to have to walk on his own."

"Thanks, man." Doug groaned. "But I'm going to need something."

Jane handed him a couple of tablets and helped him sit up. "I've got a non-opiate painkiller that'll work. Takes a little while to kick in."

Doug dry swallowed them. "Thanks." He let her push him gently back onto the table.

Jane dried her hands and put on a pair of latex gloves. She poured more peroxide on the wound. "You're not a total idiot, Mac." She dabbed at the wound with a sterile gauze and dug out a sealed pack with a disposable skin stapler. "This isn't easy to do on the stomach. I need to press. It's going to hurt." She swabbed the wound with an alcohol pad and popped open the package. "Ready? Tighten your abs if you can."

Doug laughed. "The last time I had abs was in the late nineties. Do your worst."

Jane held the edges of the wound together with one hand, pressed the stapler down and pulled the trigger.

"Fuck!" Doug lifted his head and looked at Jane. "Jesus. Sorry, that stung."

"Toughen up. Four, maybe five more to go, big guy." She punched another through his skin, and he clenched his teeth against the pain. "You're doing good." She finished affixing the staples and then applied some antibacterial cream and a sterile gauze. "Good to go."

Doug swallowed and slowly swung his feet to the floor. He pressed his hand against his side. "Tight." Cheryl stood beside him, waiting to catch him if he fell. Bob continued his vigil at the window.

"Thanks, Jane. Now get out of here. There are bad people coming," said Mac

Jane snorted. "Melodramatic much? Damn." She stripped off her latex gloves and tossed them in the bin. She started packing up her bag.

"I'm not kidding. Doug didn't cut himself shaving. The guy who did it is unconscious in the bushes behind the caravan. With a friend. And *they* have more friends who will show up shortly. Get out of here. We'll be right behind you."

"Where you going?"

Mac looked at Cheryl, who shrugged.

"We've run out of bolt holes," said Cheryl. "We'll probably just head up the coast into Queensland for now."

"And keep running?" Mac shook his head. "This will never end, you know. You need to bury him."

Jane was swivelling her head between Cheryl and Mac. "Him who?" She looked back at Cheryl again and squinted. "Hang on. I know you. You're the Prime Minister's wife. Jesus. You've got the PM after you? The media has been saying you're on vacation. Or sick. Depends on which news channel you listen to."

"Neither. He's trying to kill me."

Jane put her hands up. "Jesus on a crutch. Go to the cops."

Cheryl closed her eyes and sighed. She opened them and took a step toward Jane, nose to nose. "My husband is the Prime Minister. He has the police, local, state and federal, in his pocket. How do you think they've been so close on our heels? He has the resources of the best in the country because he's a lying, manipulative prick with a lot of favours owed. So take off. We'll disappear until we can sort it out." She stepped back beside Doug. "Let's go."

Bob put out his hand and ducked. "Hit the floor, now."

Doug, Cheryl and Mac followed suit. Jane stayed standing. "What the hell?"

Mac grabbed her hand and pulled her down to the floor. "What do you see, Bob?"

"Black SUV rolling slowly down the street." He eased his head over the sill. "They're looking for their friends. And us, by extension."

Doug groaned and pressed his hand to his side. "What's it feel like when a staple pulls out, Doc?"

Jane scooted over on the floor and lifted his shirt. Blood seeped through the gauze. "You'll live. More pressing concern is how are you guys are going to get out of here."

Bob watched the truck roll by. "They're not slowing. I think we're good."

Cheryl chewed at the inside of her cheek. "They'll know our car by now." She looked at Doug, then at Jane. "What are you driving? Can you get us out of the neighbourhood?"

Jane shook her head. "Lookout guy, is it clear?"

"My name is Bob." He raised his head a little farther. "Seems to be. How far do we have to walk?"

"I'll bring it around. Wait here." She reached for the door, then stopped. Took her bag off her shoulder and handed it to Cheryl. "Hang on to this for me. If your brother keeps leaking, there's stuff in there that'll sort him out."

Mac watched her trot down the road and around the corner.

"You trust her?" Cheryl dropped the bag on the counter. "I'm going to be really pissed if she's doing a runner."

Mac saw her vehicle, a beat-up Volkswagen Microbus, come around the corner. "She's not doing a runner, but it's going to be a tight fit."

The VW pulled to a stop outside the caravan, and Mac led Cheryl and her brothers out. "Doug in the front. We'll get in the back."

Empty coffee cups and fast food outlet bags littered the back floor. Cheryl sat in the middle with Mac on her left and Bob on the right. Doug sat in the front passenger seat in front of Mac and reclined his seat a couple of notches.

"Shit, this hurts."

Mac patted him on the shoulder. "You're good."

The last door closed, and Jane put the van in gear and pulled away. "Sitting pretty low."

Cheryl leaned forward and placed her hand on Jane's arm. "Thanks for this. Take us to—"

"My place. It's only a couple of minutes away. I need to have another look at your brother." She pulled out of the caravan park and turned left on Elizabeth Bay Drive. "What in the hell did you do to this guy that he's hunting you down?"

"Longish story. He's corrupt and abusive. I have evidence of that corruption and I've tied up a lot of his money. He's not a happy camper." She sat back in the cramped seat. "I need to figure out what to do."

Jane turned off the main road and into the village. Took a right and turned into her driveway. "Get inside. I'll call the hospital and tell them I'm sick." She looked at Mac. "Not doing this for you, Mac. I'm doing it for Cheryl and her brothers."

Chapter Twenty-Eight

"We've been by here before." Dawkins looked out of the passenger's window of the SUV. "Right? We came down this road. Past these shitty caravans. You sure this is the right place?"

The SUV rolled slowly to a stop in front of the caravan, and the driver put the vehicle in Park. "This is the last location the phones registered, boss."

Vinnie pulled up behind the SUV and got out. "Dawkins. What the fuck?"

"We're close. My guys said they thought they had something here. Phones went off the air about thirty minutes ago." Dawkins opened the caravan door and stuck his head in. "Empty." He stepped out and something crunched underfoot.

"Broken phone, Vinnie." He tossed the cracked plastic case at the short Italian. "Something doesn't feel right. Where are the rest of your guys?"

Vinnie caught the piece of broken phone and inspected it. "My guys will be here shortly. What do you think happened here?"

Dawkins squatted and looked at a dark stain on the pavement. He touched it with his index finger and rubbed his finger with his thumb. "Tacky. This is blood."

"Your guys?"

Dawkins stood, wiped his hands with a handkerchief and shrugged. "Probably. I can't reach them."

"So what the hell happened, then? This is a small woman and a couple of out-of-shape bogans."

A third vehicle rolled to a stop behind Vinnie's car, and four large men in suits stepped out. The largest specimen approached Vinnie. "What's the situation?"

"Check the bush. There's blood and a couple of boys are missing. Dawkins and I will be inside." He waddled up the steps and into the small caravan. The floor creaked under his weight. Dawkins followed him.

"They stayed here," said Dawkins. "Not for long, though." He kept his hands in his pockets and nodded at the table. "More blood. Not my guys."

Vinnie nodded and looked at the phone nailed to the wall. "There'd be a lot more mess in here if it was your guys." He picked up a tea towel from the table and flipped it over. It was caked with partially dried blood. "Although there's lots of mess. And they aren't that much ahead of us."

The big one poked his head in the door. "Found them."

He backed out, and Dawkins and Vinnie followed them into the bush. One of Dawkins' guys was still unconscious. The other was groggily sitting up, his hand on the back of his head.

Dawkins kicked the bottom of his shoe. "What the hell happened?"

"I got one of them. Gutted him."

Dawkins snorted. "Cut him, maybe. Didn't gut him. 'Cause there's no dead body around here." He kicked the bottom of the shoe harder. "How many were there? You guys were supposed to be my best."

"Her two brothers and some other bloke. Fuck." He rubbed the back of his head and winced. "The fucker kicked me."

"What did this other bloke look like?" Dawkins took out his phone and searched for a name on the internet. He held the phone out with a picture of Mac from a news story. "Like this?"

The guy reached for the phone, and Dawkins batted his hand away.

"Is that him?"

The guy nodded. "Yeah."

"You're fired." Dawkins turned to Vinnie. "The fuck is working the other side, for sure, now. I'm going to kill that arsehole. We need to find him."

Vinnie walked toward the caravan. "You've got a guy in the phone company, right?"

"Yeah, why?" He followed Vinnie in.

"That land-line. Bet they used it. They certainly aren't using their mobile phones."

Dawkins used the landline to dial his mobile, saved the number, and then made a call to Matthias.

Jane's house sat on a quiet and not quite as affluent as she'd like street in Lake Munmorah. The eaves needed cleaning, and the awning over the carport started to show rust.

Jane parked on the street and turned off the engine.

Doug looked out the window at the house. "Park in the drive? I'm not feeling like a walk, much."

Jane shook her head. "This will do."

Doug made a point of holding his side while he looked at her. "Come on."

"I hate backing up. Can't back out, won't back in. I park on the street." She opened her door and looked at Doug. "Don't push it."

They walked up the drive at the pace of the slowest. Doug. He took the three steps up to her porch and waited while she unlocked the front door. Mac, Bob and Cheryl filled the rest of the small front porch and filed in, Mac bringing up the rear.

The small living room had a sofa that Doug stretched out on and two leather chairs at angles on either side. Mac sat in one chair, and Cheryl sat in the other, both trying to stay awake. Bob stood at the window, using his finger to separate the closed slats of the venetian blind.

Jane rubbed her eye with the heel of her hand. "Who's going to tell me what in the hell is going on?"

Mac looked at Cheryl, who nodded. "You tell her, Mac. I'm tired." She leaned back in her chair and closed her eyes. "Really tired."

Mac opened his mouth to talk, and Cheryl sat forward. "My husband is a criminal." She shrugged. "Maybe I'm a bit of a criminal, too, but show me someone in politics who isn't. But he's on a whole new level. And when I told him enough was enough and that I was leaving him, he started beating on me. Like *that* was a solution. So I grabbed a bunch of his bank accounts and copies of documents and fucked off. I didn't anticipate the lengths he would go to shut me down to get his money back. I should have."

Jane took her med bag and sat beside Doug. "You're not carrying any money with you." She eased up Doug's shirt and peeled back the gauze pad. She cocked her head and looked at her handiwork.

Cheryl watched her, then sighed. She dug a thumb drive out of her pocket. "It's all on here."

Jane stopped what she was doing. "Seriously? Are you for real? Upload it all to the internet, and it'll go viral in seconds. How daft are you?"

"You think I haven't thought of that? I do that, and I become the scorned ex-wife trying to bring down a powerful man with fake news. A little might stick, but he's covered his tracks well. All he needs to do is continue to deny, and the next news cycle, it blows over. And he's the PM. He *controls* the news cycle. As soon as it looks like he's in the soup, he starts something with Indonesia or PNG or the fucking Kiwis." Cheryl leaned her head back again and closed her eyes. "I need a better plan."

Jane sat on the arm of the chair Cheryl was sitting in. "How much?"

Cheryl opened her eyes. "Huh?"

"On that thumb drive of yours. How much?"

"A smidge over twenty-three million."

"Dollars?"

"Yeah, and don't ask. I can't access it."

Jane stood and walked back to Doug to collect her medical bag. "So what's the point?"

"Technically, sure, I can get access to it. But as soon as I do, he's got me." Cheryl took a deep breath. "The money is just to piss him off. It's the documents I've got. His signature on agreements that shouldn't exist. Emails. Photos."

"I still think you should dump it on the web."

Bob spun away from the window and dove for the light switch. "Fuck." He reached for a table lamp and knocked it over. "Get the rest of the lights and get on the floor."

Jane turned off the kitchen light and sat on the floor beside Doug, who stayed on the sofa. "What in the hell is going on?"

Bob sat on the floor in the dark. The only light in the room came from the moon breaking through the clouds.

"They found us. I don't know how, but there are three SUVs just rolled up and parked on the street across the road. Don't really fit the neighbourhood." He turned to Mac. "You rat us out? I'm having second thoughts about you, mate."

Mac crawled to the window and lifted the edge of the venetian blind. "Shit." He turned and sat on the floor, his back to the wall. He thought for a moment. "I shouldn't have called you from the phone in the caravan, Jane. Sorry. Head out the back. It's going to get ugly."

Chapter Twenty-Nine

Bob looked over at Mac. "What do you mean, ugly?"

"They're not going to let us out just because we ask nice."

Bob laughed. "You're shitting me. Doug is out of commission, and the two of us aren't going to be able to take out the eight or ten Dawkins has with him." He nodded at Mac's arm. "And you're only half useful."

"So why are we hiding in the dark?"

"So they'll move on, you idiot," said Bob.

"Who's the idiot? They know where we are." Mac checked the time. "It's late. It'll happen very soon."

Cheryl stood and turned on a light. "Mac's right. This is it, then. I hoped it would end better. Call an ambulance for Doug. I'm going to talk to Dawkins and stop this bullshit. You don't need to get hurt because of me."

Mac peered out the window. "Vinnie's with him."

Cheryl ran to his side and peered through the blinds. "Shit. Vinnie." She backed up and turned slowly in the front room. "Is there a back way out of here?"

"Out of the house, yes. But into a fenced yard."

"Hey, Jane, where's your knives?" asked Bob.

"We're not fighting them, Bob, okay?" Mac scratched under the edge of his cast. "You're right. We're outnumbered 8 to 1 and a half, and I'm not drunk enough to take on odds like that." He stood beside Cheryl. "Vinnie is just a fat fuck with body odour. What's the deal?"

"He's a psychopath. My husband's pet psychopath. Dawkins, I can handle, but Vinnie will hurt me until I wish I were dead."

Mac's mobile phone rang. He pulled it from his back pocket and stared at it. It rang again.

"You going to answer that?" asked Cheryl.

"It's a burner. Nobody knows the number." He jabbed the answer button and pressed it to his head. "Durridge."

"Of course it is." Dawkins' voice came through the phone a split second after Mac heard a faint version outside. "You made a big fucking mistake, Mac."

"You're a cliché. What is this supposed to prove? Do you want us to come out? Then what? There's witnesses all over the place."

"I know a guy who will help them adjust their memories."

Mac laughed. "A massive cliché. Fuck off, Dawkins. I'm going to hang up and call the cops. They might be a while. Not the greatest service out here. But they'll show up eventually. You'll have plenty of time to fuck off. Or not. Your choice."

"Oh, we're not going anywhere. And save your minutes. You won't need to call the police. They'll be here shortly." Dawkins hung up.

Mac dropped his phone on the counter. "So much for anonymity. So there's a way out the back, Jane?"

"Like I said, into a fenced yard. What's the hurry? Call the cops and wait them out."

"I don't think we're going to have that luxury." Mac headed to the back of the house and saw two shadowy shapes run through the backyard. "Sit rep out front, Bob. What's going on there?"

"They're spreading out." Bob moved to a side window. "Oh, shit."

Mac watched one of the men in the backyard flick a lighter a couple of times and ignite a rag sticking out of the end of a bottle. "Fucking hell. Cheryl, you've really pissed off the wrong people." The bottle landed on the back porch, and fire spread across the door. "Bob, the front?"

He heard a crash of breaking glass and a loud *whoomp* as a wall of flames covered the front door. Two almost simultaneous smashes covered the front of the house in flame. The windows cracked, and the blinds started melting.

Bob helped Doug to his feet off the sofa and ran to the back of the house, Cheryl by his side.

Jane grabbed at Cheryl. "You're not going to get out that way. Upstairs."

Mac coughed as smoke filled the room. "That's stupid. Smoke rises. We need to find a way out of here."

"Yeah, get the fuck upstairs. Go." Jane stood to one side as Cheryl and Bob helped Doug.

Mac followed. His eyes watered. He wiped them with a sleeve. "You have a plan, I take it? Upstairs will be filled with smoke in a minute or two. We open the windows, and it'll be a chimney."

Jane pushed him up the stairs. "I had the brains in our relationship, Mac. Move it." She yelled up the stairs. "Second door on the right."

Mac staggered up the stairs and followed Cheryl and her brothers into the bedroom. Jane followed and slammed the door shut. She grabbed a quilt off the bed and jammed it along the bottom of the door.

Mac looked at her. "Are you fucking nuts? Unless the walls are made of fireproof material, we'll burn to death in here. And if they *are* fireproof, we'll cook like we're in an oven. Because we'll be in a fucking oven."

Jane shook her head and strode to the other side of the bedroom. She flung open floor-length drapes to a sliding door leading out to a small deck. She put her hand on the latch to open the door, and Mac leapt forward and grabbed her hand.

"Open that, and we're in the middle of a chimney."

Jane looked at him and shook her head again. She nodded toward the door. "Why do you think I just ruined my best bedspread? No air is getting in under the door." She flipped the latch and opened the door. "No chimney." Flames licked against the railing along the floor. "This isn't going to be easy."

She pointed to her left. "My neighbour's bedroom balcony. An easy jump on a good day. It's going to be a challenge under the circumstances."

Mac leaned out the door and looked. The balcony was the same size as Jane's, roughly three metres wide and two deep. A small wicker table and two matching chairs occupied most of the space. The near railing was three metres away. "What's a good day for you? That's tough on any day."

"No choice," said Jane. She gestured to Cheryl. "You first. You think you can do this?"

The flames licked higher against the outside walls of the small house. Cheryl looked down. "Like I have a choice. You've done this?"

Jane smiled. "I've popped over to Mark's place a time or two this way."

"Really? Mark?"

"Shut up, Mac." Jane took Cheryl by the forearm. "Commit to it. It's not that far. We'll be right behind you. If he's still in his house, tell him to get the fuck out before the fire spreads."

"How is Doug going to get across?"

"We'll work something out. Go, Cheryl."

Jane helped her balance on the railing, hanging on to the eaves trough for balance. "Dive for it. Commit."

Cheryl squatted down on the railing, then launched herself forward. She cleared the far railing, smashed into the table, and landed on the deck floor. She was down for a moment, then pulled herself up.

She lifted the table over the railing and dropped it into the backyard. She threw one chair over the railing and had lifted the second when a man ran onto the deck with an extendable ladder.

Jane yelled across the gap. "Mark. Thank God."

He stretched the ladder between the balconies. Mac grabbed an end and held it in place. "Get the rest of them across, Jane. Quick. This place is going up."

The heat was getting uncomfortable. Mac held the ladder firmly and turned his head away from the smoke. A draft of smoke enveloped his head, and he shook with coughs. The ladder sagged as Doug crawled, inching across on his hands and knees.

"Hurry," said Cheryl, holding out a hand to help him off the ladder.

Bob pushed Jane in front of him. "You go next."

"Chivalry always surprises me." Jane jumped up on the ladder and walked across. Bob followed. Flames licked up the wall. The railing was hot, and the ladder was getting hot, also. Mac pulled his sleeves over his hands and crawled onto the ladder. The rungs dug into his knees. He inched along and felt the ladder shake under his weight. He crawled a few more steps, and the ladder bumped again. He looked over his shoulder. The flames were up the side of the house and the balcony was canted at an angle away from the house. He redoubled his efforts and grabbed Mark's balcony railing as Jane's balcony fell away. He scrambled and pulled himself over.

"Mark, you're a lifesaver. What are you still doing in this house? We all need to get out of here." He looked back at Jane's house, now fully engaged. He followed Mark into the bedroom. The television was on, and Linda Carmody was reporting from the scene of a house fire in Lake Munmorah. A dozen cop cars and a couple of fire trucks were her backdrop.

Mac pointed at the TV. "They got here pretty fast."

"The fire's been going for about thirty minutes now. If it burns, it earns." He ushered Mac out of the bedroom, turning off the television as he passed. "And we need to get out of the house. Mandatory evacuation."

"Everyone else?"

"Downstairs. Waiting for you. Won't go outside without you."

Mac ran down the stairs. The house was laid out in a mirror image of Jane's. Cheryl and her brothers were in the living room. Jane left the kitchen with a glass of water and handed it to Doug. "He's not well. We need to get him to a hospital. There's not a lot more I can do. I think he needs surgery."

"I've got this deja vu feeling all over again." Mac looked out the window. He spotted the three black SUVs parked on the far side of the street, illuminated by the flashing emergency lights. "Mark, can we get out the back? Are you fenced in, too? I didn't notice."

Mark looked out the window, then glanced at Jane. "There's a gate at the back that leads to a path to the beach."

"I know it. But my van's on the road," said Jane. "There's a dirt road back there."

Mac thought for a second. "That should be good. Nobody out there has seen you."

"I'll walk around and get it once we get out of here."

"Then let's go. We'll sort Doug out." Mac clapped Mark on the shoulder. "Do me a favour, mate? Don't tell anyone you saw us, okay? We'll explain later."

Chapter Thirty

Dawkins had parked half a block down the street. Wilson was in the driver's seat, Dawkins slumped down in the passenger's seat peering out the side window. He watched the fire start, his men run back into their respective vehicles before the neighbours popped out, and the arrival of the fire and police. Locals gathered just beyond the working perimeter, gawking and worrying about the fire spreading to their respective homes.

Dawkins motioned for Wilson to move the SUV forward. Wilson pressed the ignition button, and the SUV rumbled to life. He eased the truck forward until it was directly across the street from the house, parked on the wrong side of the road, driver's side to the curb.

"Think it's safe, boss? We should get out of here. You don't want to get caught up in this."

"Shut off the engine. We're just another car on the street. I'm staying until the ashes are cold, and I'm sure that bitch and everyone she was with is a pile of charred bone."

Wilson shrugged and leaned back, closing his eyes. "You're the boss. Wake me when you're satisfied."

Dawkins settled in the passenger's seat to watch the fire. It was a primal force, cleansing, an element of nature. It is great for destroying evidence. Flames engulfed the house. His men had told him the back was fenced off, and nobody had come out the front. His problem was over, and he would be handsomely paid for his efforts. And with Mac gone, there was nothing coming back to him.

Two engines and a dozen men were fighting a losing fight. A couple of cop cars, red and blue lights flashing across the neighbour's houses, were moving what little traffic there was at night through a contraflow with well-practised precision. Local media were telling the breathless public at thirty-minute intervals the state of the fire.

A third engine arrived, and three hardy-looking young men jumped out and manned a hose, helping quench the flames. There were three hoses now, and the addition of the third finally seemed to impact the fire. Dawkins assumed the main focus of the attack at this point was containing the inferno to the single house. The structure was beyond saving.

Neighbours were moving their vehicles at the direction of the police. Only vehicles on the same side of the road at this point. Dawkins sank deeper in his seat and watched the process. Bathrobe-clad people ran to their vehicles and moved them down the street, around the corner or across the street. An old VW microbus that didn't look like it needed to be moved, and even if it did would be no loss to the owner if it lit up, sped away around the corner in a cloud of exhaust.

Dawkins looked in the passenger side mirror at the two black SUVs behind him. Too conspicuous. He depressed the microphone on a handy-talkie.

"Boys, head home. This is done. I'll hang around a bit."

Squawks of acknowledgement were drowned out by the roar of the fire as the roof collapsed. Dawkins' face was illuminated by the bright orange flare, and he slid down in his seat.

Wilson opened an eye. "Maybe we should get out of here too, Dawks." Two more police cars pulled into the street. "It's getting busy."

Dawkins slowly sat straighter and looked out the door window at the police cars. "No. Hang tight." He popped open the door and approached the cordon.

Chapter Thirty-One

The microbus rolled to a stop on the side of the dirt road. The passenger door popped open, and Jane yelled for them to get in. Cheryl held the door while Mac and Mark helped Doug up to the front seat, and then the rest piled in the back.

"No problems?" asked Mac.

"I don't think so. Three black SUVs parked the wrong way on the other side of the road. They looked pretty obvious. They didn't seem to be paying attention. A couple of them left just after I did. I thought they were following me, but they peeled off and headed to the M1. Nobody behind me."

Mac closed the door to the back. "We need to get out of here."

"Where?"

Doug groaned. "I don't feel good." He lifted his hand from his side. It was covered with blood. "I think I popped a couple of more stitches."

"Staples. Let me look." She peeled up his shirt. The gauze was red, saturated with blood. She reached between the seats and grabbed her medical bag. "Can't be subtle now. Hold that shirt up." She tore open a handful of gauze pads and pressed them on the wound. "Hold these there."

Doug pressed his hand against the pads and the wound. "Fuuuuck, this hurts."

"You'll live." Jane opened a roll of gauze and put one end under his hand. "Lean forward." She reached around him and rolled half a dozen layers around his stomach and tied it off.

She looked back at Mac and shook her head.

Mac nodded. "Floor it, Jane. To the hospital."

Jane skewed the microbus to a shuddering halt in front of the A&E Entrance of the Wyong hospital. Doug winced and opened the front passenger door and slid out into Mac's arms.

"Hang on, mate. We're here."

Jane ran ahead for help. Bob and Mark ran around the van to help Mac support Doug. They stagger-stepped, Cheryl hovering.

Doug held a hand to his side and winced. "I'm not dying, guys. Take it easy." He weakly shrugged off the help and tried walking on his own, sagging against the doorframe. "Never mind. Help me. Shit, I'm as weak as a fucking baby. How much blood did I lose?"

"Most of it, by the mess." Mac put one of Doug's arms over his shoulder, and Bob the other, and they walked him into the triage nurse's office. Cheryl was in full force.

"You *do not* call the police, and you *do not* call my husband. My brother was injured in an accident *at home*. He is currently under Jane's care, and I insist that she remain his primary physician."

Jane placed a hand on Cheryl's arm. "I've got this, Cheryl. I know the staff here. Doug will be in good hands." She turned as Mac and Bob arrived with her patient. She grabbed a wheelchair and made sure it was locked open. "Sit. I'll be with you in a minute, Doug. The rest of you, there's a coffee shop next door. Get a bite, stay out of trouble, and I'll keep you updated as Doug gets patched up."

Cheryl leaned down and kissed Doug on the cheek. "You get better. Do as they say."

Mac carried the tray of take-away coffee and pastries to the table. Cheryl sat between Mark and Bob. Mac set the tray on the table and sat across from them. He handed out the coffee. "Long black, that's you, Bob. Soy latte for Cheryl and a cappuccino for our hero, Mark." He took the second long black and placed it in front of himself. "Plate full of sticky buns for immediate sugar rush." He scratched at the stubble on his jaw. It was getting itchy. "We need a plan."

Mark looked from Mac to Bob and Cheryl. "Plan? Plan for what?"

Mac looked at Cheryl and Bob, trying to read their expression. "I don't know this guy. It's up to you how much we tell him."

Cheryl thought for a minute then shrugged. "He saved our arses and didn't hand us over to that little fuck, Dawkins. I trust him." She took a deep breath. "So, what's the plan?"

Mac yawned. "I don't think Dawkins knows we made it out. We're dead, as far as he knows. We need to use that as long as we can. He'll figure it out eventually."

"We're no further ahead," said Cheryl. "Still up against Vinnie and my husband at every turn."

Mark took a deep breath and slowly exhaled. "Not really any of my business, but you're dead, right? They won't have any idea what you're doing."

Cheryl shook her head. "Dawkins will suss that out pretty quick."

"He'll have called Vinnie to tell him everyone is dead, right? He strikes me as the impulsive sort."

"Probably," said Cheryl. "But he's also thorough. He'll stay there until the fireys have finished and done a body count. He'll know for sure in a couple of hours."

"Then we've got a couple of hours. I know someone at a local news station who would love a scoop like this."

Cheryl shook her head. "We can't wait a couple of hours. We need to make sure that Dawkins doesn't report back to Vinnie." She took a bite of pastry, a pecan plait, and wiped her mouth. "We've got to head back to Jane's place."

Mac choked on his coffee. "What?"

Bob nodded. "I agree. Dawkins is probably still there. If we're going to take him down, that's where we'll do it."

"He's got a lot of muscle," said Mac. "Muscle that put your brother in the hospital."

"No, no. Jane watched the others leave, remember. I'm concerned about the crowd of cops and fireys there. He'll be low-key. But it keeps *us* from being too overt." She took another bite of her pastry. "He's convinced he won. We are all dead, as far as he knows."

Mac shook his head. "I still think he'll have left by now."

Bob leaned forward. "Listen to my sister. He'll be there." He sat back emphatically, almost tipping back in his chair. He smacked his head against the wall behind him. "Fuck."

Mac laughed. "Okay, she's the boss." He looked out of the coffee shop back toward the hospital waiting room. "Doug?"

Cheryl finished her coffee and stood. "Let's see."

Back at the triage station, Cheryl tapped on the screen to get someone's attention. Bob stood beside her, Mac slightly behind. Mark, the friendly neighbour, stood back, unsure of his status.

Jason poked his head around the corner, smiled at Cheryl and exited from behind through a staff door. He saw Mac and glanced back at Cheryl. Then back to Mac. "You okay? That cast looks like it's had a bit of wear and tear over the past, what, twenty-four hours?

"I've been better. That's not why we're here. We came in with Doug Collins. What's the status?"

"Jane is stitching him up. It's not that serious unless there's an infection. It was a pretty ragged gash. The guy's going to have a noticeable scar."

"But he'll be okay?" asked Cheryl.

"Most likely. He's in good hands. Jane knows what she's doing. It'll be another couple of hours before he's ready to go." Jason shrugged apologetically. "Make yourself comfortable."

Mac looked at the plastic chairs. "I say we get out of here, sort out Dawkins and come back. We won't be that long. Maybe Doug can wait for *us* for a little bit."

"I don't know," said Bob.

Cheryl nodded, her mind made up. "Mac is right. Let's take Dawkins off the map." She turned to Mark. "You with us?"

Mark looked over his shoulder, then back at Mac, Cheryl and Bob. "Me?"

"We need all the help we can get," said Mac. "You're a pretty big unit. Might come in handy."

Jason shook his head and headed back to the triage centre. "I don't want to hear any of this."

A smile slowly spread across Mark's face. "Haven't been in a fight in a while." He smacked a fist into his left hand. "Might be fun."

Cheryl stepped forward and pressed an index finger against his chest. "This isn't playtime. If we get into it, Dawkins and his boys will be trying to kill us. Including you." She paused and looked into his eyes. "You up for *that*?"

The smile faded slightly and his chest puffed out almost imperceptibly. "Fuck, yeah."

Mac clapped his hands together. "Okay then. We need a plan of attack."

Chapter Thirty-Two

It had been over an hour since Dawkins' men had lit Jane's house on fire, and the firemen were finally getting it under control. The fire's roar had ebbed. The fireys primary concern now was keeping the fire from spreading to the neighbours' homes.

A Rural Fire Service car was parked beside one of the engines, the chief standing beside it surveying the fight, walkie in hand.

Dawkins leaned his mouth close to the fire chief's ear. "So what do you think started it? Electrical?"

The chief looked at him, then back at his men working the flames.

Dawkins stuck out his hand. "Lawrence Dawkins, Dawkins Investigation Services. I have a particular interest in the cause."

The chief looked at Dawkins' hand, then shook it. "Wally Pace. Chief Wally Pace. What's your interest? This your home?"

Dawkins shook his head. "I was retained to find someone, and my most current information is that she was in there. Any information about bodies in the house?"

Pace pointed at the house. "We tried a sweep, but this place was fully involved when the first truck arrived. And it's still well alight. How the fuck would we know if anybody's in there?" He placed the walkie on the car's bonnet and picked up a pen and clipboard. "Dawkins right? Who was it you were looking for?"

Dawkins took a deep breath and pulled out his wallet. He fished out a picture of his wife and showed it to Pace. "Her name is Lynda Carver. Her husband thinks she's messing around on him. I tracked her here. The fire was going when I got here, too."

Pace took the photo and looked at it for a second before handing it back. He scribbled the name on the clipboard. "Well, if she's in there, she certainly doesn't look like that now. Horrible way to go."

"Any preliminary indication on the cause of the fire?"

"More than preliminary. There are clear signs of accelerant on the front. Neighbours across the street said they saw a couple of guys in black throwing lit bottles at the house. Maybe your jealous husband. Or friends of his." Pace looked around. "There's a cop around here somewhere you should talk to. They'll be starting the investigation as soon as the arson team can get in to do a thorough look-through." Pace looked at his watch. "By dawn, I guess. Too dark now, anyway. Even if the fire was out. We'd need one of those bright fucking lights they use on night road construction jobs. Not in the budget. Where'd that cop go?"

Dawkins stuffed the photo in his wallet. He clapped Pace on the shoulder. "You stay focussed on the fire. I'll find him."

Pace dropped the clipboard on the bonnet of his car. "You do that."

Dawkins swore under his breath and angled back toward his SUV. He'd almost reached his truck when he saw Carmody and her TV crew packing up. He redirected toward them. "Hey, I've seen you on TV, right?"

Linda Carmody brushed hair out of her eyes and stifled a yawn. "I'm surprised you recognise me. I'm a mess. I'm flattered."

"Hard to miss you. Quite a fire, right? Good footage?"

Linda scowled. "It's a tragedy for someone. Thank God the fireys have kept the adjacent houses safe."

Dawkins nodded sagely. "Would be terrible if someone was in there, but I heard it was empty. It's just stuff, right?"

Linda paid more attention. "Where did you hear it was empty? The neighbours said four or five people entered about half an hour before the fire started. None of them saw anyone leave."

"Four or five?"

"That's what was said. I have no reason not to believe them. Until now. Why do you think it was empty? What did you hear? From who?"

Dawkins waved away the question. "I'm probably wrong. You're the journalist. I'll take your word for it. I hope you're wrong, though." He walked back to his truck and climbed in.

"So, boss. We outta here?" Wilson poked the button on the dash and started the vehicle.

"No. I need to be sure. Absolutely one hundred per cent sure."

Wilson stopped the engine. "And you're not."

Dawkins shook his head. "Almost. Maybe eighty per cent. Witnesses saw five go in. Nobody saw them leave. And we've been here all along, and we haven't seen anyone leave. At least I didn't."

"Me either. So what's the problem?"

Dawkins scratched at his chin. "If five people had been in there, at least one of them would have tried to make it out. No sign of anyone. Doesn't sit right with me. It falls into the 'too easy' pile."

"Dangerous, boss. If they're not in there, they're somewhere else, and we're sitting on our arses doing nothing."

"Start the engine. Warm it up. I need a couple of hours sleep." He looked at the time on the dash. "Wake me at 6:00 a.m."

Mac was driving the VW Microbus. The flashing red and blue lights made finding the house easy. Mac turned off the headlights and slowly rolled up the street. The house was still burning. "Jane is going to be pissed."

Cheryl tapped his arm. "Stop. That's one of Dawkins' trucks at the kerb." She glanced at the fire. "Don't worry. Jane'll be fine. She seems like one of those sensible people who buys insurance. We've got more pressing problems."

Mark stuck his head between the front seats. "There are cops here. We're not going to anything right now, right?"

Cheryl looked around, checking vehicles. "Jane was right. There's only one of the SUVs here. Dawkins figures he's got us all."

"He's not completely convinced, or he'd be gone, too." Mac checked his watch. "He's waiting until daylight to check for remains. Very thorough."

Cheryl sat back in her seat. "We're waiting, too. Until the cops are gone. Only Dawkins here, without his apes, makes it much easier." She adjusted in her seat. "Make yourself comfortable. It's going to be a while."

"A bit of time to sort out a plan, then," said Mac.

Chapter Thirty-Three

Mac tapped on the centre console. "Mark. They're leaving."

The local yawned from the back seat. "Got it." He leaned between the front seats and watched the last police car leave. "Haven't had a fight in years."

"Hopefully, we can avoid one today." Mac opened the centre console and extracted a handful of nylon cable ties. "But you're a big lad. Consider it an aerobic workout, should it come to that." He closed the console. "Go."

Mark got out of the back of the car and walked past the SUV toward his house. A single fire engine was still there, with the crew stowing their equipment. Jane's house was a charred shell, small tendrils of smoke illuminated by the truck's flashing lights. Mac watched Mark stop and talk to the fireman, pointing at his house. Police tape prevented anyone from entering Jane's property, but access was granted to Mark. The fire truck pulled away as Mark entered.

Mac watched him. "Step one successful." He looked at Cheryl. "You good?"

"It's going to take everything I've got to not kill that motherfucker."

Mac nodded. "You're good."

Cheryl nodded toward Mark's house. He was coming down the front stairs, something in his hand. "Step one complete."

Mark walked down the middle of the road toward them, passing by Dawkins' vehicle. He glanced in the window and kept walking to the car. Mac rolled down the window, and he leaned in. "Dawkins is a little shit, right? Short, sandy hair?"

"That's him," said Mac. "Is he with anyone?"

"He's in the passenger's seat. A bigger guy is behind the wheel. Dawkins looks like he's asleep. Driver isn't that alert." He held up the object in his hand. A long handled barbecue fork, sharp tines glistening in the light. "Will this do?"

"Perfect." Mac looked in the back seat. "Bob. You ever meet Dawkins?"

"No, but he's probably got my picture."

"He won't recognise you. You go up the driver's side, Cheryl behind you. Mark, head up the passenger's side. I'll stay behind you. Close to the side of the vehicle to block the side mirrors. Fifty-fifty chance the doors are unlocked. If they're not, Mark, knock on the window and do the suspicious neighbour act." He handed the cable ties to Mark. "Trade you."

Bob got out of the back of the microbus and stood by the front fender and motioned for his sister to get out. Mark handed the weapon to Mac, took the cable ties and took up a position at the other fender.

"Okay," said Mac. "Quick and clean."

Mark walked up the passenger's side of the SUV with Mac tucked in behind him. Bob and Cheryl walked up the driver's side. Mark rested his hand on the door handle.

"Now!" said Mac.

Mark yanked the door open and Mac lunged in, holding the fork to Dawkins' neck. On the other side of the vehicle, Bob had pulled open the door and dragged the driver onto the ground.

Dawkins looked through the open driver's door at Cheryl. Bob and Wilson were out of sight, but the sound of fists hitting flesh was loud.

Mac pressed the tines into Dawkins' neck, breaking the skin. "You going to fight back?"

The little detective slowly raised his hands. "You're a fucking dead man."

"Not today."

"The day is young. Really young."

Mark cracked his knuckles and laughed. "You almost burned down my house, man. I want to shove that fork straight through."

Cheryl lunged in from the driver's side and punched Dawkins on the side of the head, driving him into the fork. "Arsehole!"

The fork tines only penetrated a couple of millimetres, enough for him to bleed. Mac pulled back, and Dawkins slapped his hand to his neck. "You son of a bitch."

"You'll live. Get out, slowly."

Dawkins growled something under his breath and lowered himself out of the truck. He stood facing Mac, his head up to Mac's chest.

"You really are a little fucker. Turn around. Put your hands behind you." Mac gave him a shove.

Dawkins stared at Mac for a second, then turned. Halfway through the turn, he lashed out, kicking back with his foot, aimed at Mac's groin. Mac grabbed the foot and pulled. Dawkins fell forward, bouncing his forehead of the running board. He stayed on the ground, stunned.

Mac handed the fork to Mark and searched Dawkins. He found what he was looking for in his front right pocket. He took a look at the cell phone and slid it in his pocket. Mark handed him a couple of cable ties. He fastened Dawkins' wrists and ankles and rolled him over on his back. "Are you awake?"

A cut across Dawkins forehead was leaking blood. "Fuck you."

Mac toe-punted him in the ribs. "Into the truck you go." He opened the back door, dragged him in and placed him on the floor. "Maybe we'll come back for you." He slammed the door shut and walked to the other side of the truck.

Bob had just finished cable-tying the driver and was dragging him to the back of the SUV. The driver's face was bent and bloody. Mac opened the tailgate and helped Bob lift. The driver was a dead weight. "You kill him?"

"Not even close. But he's going to hurt when he comes to. Should we gag them?"

Mac shook his head. "Too much chance of him suffocating. Don't want to kill him."

"I do." Cheryl slammed the tailgate shut. "Now what?"

"Grab the keys out of the ignition." Mac held up Dawkins' phone. "We head up the food chain." He thought for a second, then entered the passcode to unlock it.

"How do you know that?"

"He's got crappy security. Watched him unlock it when his thumbprint didn't work. Too much condensation on the outside of a can of diet cola." He opened the messaging app and scrolled

272

until he found a message from Vinnie. "What would we tell him?"

Chapter Thirty-Four

Vinnie sat in his lounge room in an overstuffed chair with a glass of whiskey in his fist. The television was on, and the volume was low. There had been very little news about the house fire in Lake Munmorah. He looked at his phone, picked it up, and then put it back down again. As soon as it touched the table beside his chair it rang. He started, then answered. "Vinnie speaking. This you?"

The Prime Minister spoke on the other end. "What's going on? I expected an update by now."

"Dawkins contacted me a couple of hours ago to tell me the targets were trapped in a fire. Emergency services were on the scene, but it didn't look like anybody had gotten out."

There was a sigh on the other end of the line. "So it's over then?"

Vinnie leaned back and closed his eyes. "Not a hundred per cent. Dawkins is waiting until the fire's out so he can confirm there were bodies."

"So when's that going to be?"

"Don't know. I'm expecting something from him any minute."

"Call him and let me know what's going on. I'll wait."

Vinnie looked at the phone and the disconnected call. He scrolled to recent calls and called Dawkins. It rang until it went to voicemail. "Dawkins, call me. Boss needs an update. Stat."

He dropped the phone on the side table and picked up his drink. The news cycle was coming around again. The fire coverage was less than the previous time. In an hour or so, it would be replaced by something else. "I'll fucking handle it myself next time."

The time on the news channel told him it was a little after 4:00 am. He was bone tired. His eyes started drifting closed when his phone buzzed on the table. It was a message from Dawkins: "*Can't talk. Stand by. I think I've received confirmation the bodies were in the fire.*"

Vinnie called the number. It again rang until it went to voicemail. "Listen, you little fuck. Answer your goddamned phone, or I'll personally track you down and break your tiny fingers." He stabbed the 'End' button and dropped it on the table. "Little shit."

A new bulletin flashed across the screen. He turned up the volume. Someone named Linda Carmody was breathlessly reporting from in front of what looked like a burned-out house.

"*This is Linda Carmody with an update from the house fire we've been following in Lake Munmorah. The house has been razed. Witness reports show that there were four or five people in the house when it went up. Fire investigators have told me there are no signs that anyone alive attempted to leave the house, but a fence in the backyard has been broken. Investigations are continuing, but they are fairly certain the house wasn't empty when it went up.*

"*Additionally, officials have reported that it appears there were several initiation points around the house. In effect, the house was lit on fire intentionally. Investigators are continuing work. I will be sure to update you as soon as new information arises. This is Linda Carmody of Central Coast News, reporting live from the scene."*

The station played footage from earlier in the evening, when the fire had just started. Vinnie poured another two fingers into his glass and sat in front of the television. Carmody's cameras played across the fire to the neighbouring homes. The house on the left looked like a mirror image of the one on the right, only a few metres away. Vinnie marvelled at the fact it didn't catch. "Those fireys are pretty good."

A glint of fire off something shiny between the houses made Vinnie sit forward in his chair. He grabbed the remote and rewound the video. He advanced it a frame at a time until he saw a flash of something between the houses. He kneeled on the floor right in front of the screen and continued to advance a frame at a time.

It was clear at the slow speed. A few seconds after the flash between the houses, from right to left, a ladder extended from left to right. It was impossible to make out who each blob crossing the ladder was, but it was obvious people were shuffling across. He counted four, plus whoever jumped across at first. They all got out. He stood and threw the remote across the room. It shattered into a cloud of plastic fragments when it hit the wall. "Motherfucker!"

He grabbed the phone and redialled. Again to Dawkins' voicemail. "They got out. They *fucking* got out. I hope to fucking hell you have them in your sights. Answer my *fucking* calls, or never work in this town again."

Chapter Thirty-Five

Mac listened to the voicemail. "Vinnie is some pissed. Dawkins might have a bit of a climb to get his business back on track." He leaned against the wall. "He knows we weren't in the house. Plans need to change."

"How'd he find out?"

"I don't know, Cheryl." Mac looked at the phone in his hand. "But he doesn't know Dawkins is out of commission."

They were in Mark's house. Bob was asleep on the sofa. Mark was in the kitchen making coffee.

Cheryl paced the lounge room floor. "Any ideas?"

Mark called from the kitchen. "Coffee, anyone? I will die if I don't get some in me."

Mac smiled. "Cheryl, can you call the hospital and get Jane on the phone? Hand me the keys first." He caught them from Cheryl and tossed them to Mark. "Mark, thanks for the save. Bring the truck around and back it into your drive. We need to store our friends somewhere if we're going to be driving the truck."

Bob sat up on the sofa. "Why are we driving the truck? Jane's wheels work fine."

"Vinnie needs to think it's Dawkins driving up on him. Go help Mark. That driver is kind of hefty."

Cheryl handed the phone to Mac. "Jane."

"Thanks." Mac walked off to a corner. "Jane, how's Doug doing?"

"He's resting. He needed a handful of real stitches. There was a bit of infection." She paused. "What's going on, Mac? Cheryl sounded weird. You get this sorted out yet?"

"One step at a time. I need Doug to die."

Vinnie looked out over the water. The dim pre-dawn grey sucked the colours from the landscape. He had that hollow, over-tired feeling that he was both familiar with and thought was in his past. He called Dawkins again. It rang to voicemail. "Dawkins, give me an update. Now. I need to brief the boss, and right now, the briefing will be 'Dawkins fucked up'. Call."

He stood on his deck and watched the sky lighten. It was going to be a long day. He could feel it in his bones. He sent a message to his driver. *"Get the car ready. We're heading north."*

He received an incoming message almost as fast as he had hit send. It was from Dawkins. *"Sorry, been off the grid. Check the news. Now."*

Vinnie sighed, walked into the lounge room, and turned on the television. He looked for the buttons on the TV to turn up the volume, regretting the impulse to shatter the remote. He landed on a local news station.

Linda Carmody was standing in front of a small regional hospital. It looked like a live shot. Vinnie fumbled with buttons so he could hear what she was saying.

"This is Linda Carmody of Central Coast News, reporting from the Wyong Hospital. The news from last night's fire in Lake Munmorah doesn't get much better. One victim, a thirty-four-year-old Douglas Collins, has died of complications from third-degree burns and smoke inhalation. Four other victims are currently in critical condition, two of whom are not expected to survive. Arson investigators have told me that preliminary indications are that the fire was deliberately set. Police are treating the house as a crime scene."

Vinnie called Dawkins' number. Voicemail. "Jesus motherfucking Christ why can't you answer your fucking phone? They're in the hospital. Great. They can't survive. Meet me there."

His phone responded with an immediate text. *"Can't talk. In the hospital. Meet me here. Low key. Security all over the place. I have a nurse on the inside."*

Vinnie threw on a clean set of clothes and tracked down his driver. "I'm in a rush. Need to get to the Wyong hospital. Do you know where it is?"

His driver held up his phone. "If it's in Australia, we can drive there." He opened a navigation app. "Wyong?" He tapped a couple of things on his phone. "Hour and a half."

"Faster if you can."

Mac handed out bacon and egg rolls and coffee. "We've got about an hour to get to the hospital. Vinnie will be expecting Dawkins, and he'll be pissed that Dawkins hasn't been answering his calls. I told him to come light, so he'll at most have a driver with him."

"We hope," said Bob.

Mac nodded and took a bite. He thought while he chewed. "We've got surprise on our side. And Cheryl's motivated enough to kill him single-handedly. But we don't want him dead."

"Says who?" asked Cheryl.

"Trust me. Not worth it." Mac wiped his face and downed his coffee. "We need your help, Mark, but if you don't want to come, I completely understand."

"The arsehole is behind the fire, right? Almost flattened my place, too? I'm in. Jane wouldn't have it any other way."

"Finest kind. Eat up. We need to set ourselves up at the hospital."

Vinnie's car pulled off the Pacific Highway and into the Wyong Hospital grounds.

"We're here, boss. Where do you want me to go?" asked his driver.

Vinnie yawned and looked around. "Keep an eye peeled for a big black SUV. Dawkins likes to think he's Secret Service or something. Napoleon complex. The short little fucker."

They rolled through the first parking lot, which was mostly empty. No SUVs were visible. Vinnie called Dawkins and hung up when he got a voice mail.

A text came in almost immediately. *"Heading out of the hospital in a couple of minutes. Parked in the far lot by the back. I'll meet you there."*

Vinnie read the message, then looked up and scanned the far parking lot. He pointed. "There. At the back. Staying out of sight, I guess. Park beside them."

The driver nodded assent and pulled into the parking lot. There were more empty spots than occupied ones. "Leave a couple of spots between us. Don't want to make it look obvious."

"Right."

The driver parked three spots from the SUV. It was to Vinnie's left. He looked out of the window at it. Dark-tinted windows obscured his view. He sent a text. *"We're here. You in your car?"*

"Hang on. Coming out in a couple of minutes."

Vinnie shook his head. "You know what Dawkins looks like, right? Little smug fuck? Go in there and roust him. I'm tired. This needs to end. Bring him to my car."

"Sure thing, boss."

Vinnie angled the rear-view mirror and watched his driver lope back toward the hospital. He didn't see Mark and Mac approach his car from the blind side.

Mac grabbed the door handle and pulled the door open and Mark grabbed Vinnie's arm and pulled him onto the pavement.

"What the fuck do you think you're doing?" Vinnie squinted up at Mac. "You? I should have fucking known." He stood and started to dust off his clothes. "You're de—"

Cheryl ran up and slugged him on the side of his neck. "Shut up."

Mac scanned the parking lot. "Into the trees. We don't want an audience."

"Over my dead body." Vinnie grabbed Mac by the front of the shirt and started pushing. "You're going to wish you were never born."

Mac grabbed Vinnie's fingers and pulled them back, breaking one of them. Bob and Mark pulled at his arms and, between the three of them, wrestled Vinnie into the trees beside the parking lot.

"What the fuck do you think you're going to do, hey? Jesus Christ, you're making a huge mistake," said Vinnie. "You're fucking dead meat."

Mac and Mark held an arm each and let Cheryl and Bob go at Vinnie. Cheryl first. Elbow to the side of the head, Bob booted him in the nuts. It was kind of noisy, but there were very few people around.

After a couple of minutes, most of which Vinnie was unconscious, Mac held out a hand. "Okay, okay. We really don't want to kill him."

"We do."

"But we won't." He let go, and Vinnie slumped to the ground. Mac went through his suit pockets until he found his phone. Grabbed the fat man's thumb to unlock it, then changed the security password.

He dropped Vinnie's hand and toe-punted him in the ribs. "Clean him of any ID. Strip him of every possible thing that could be used to identify him. I'll move the truck over. We'll load him in the back and dump him at the hospital door. Jane will handle it from there." He dug through Vinnie's pockets again, then looked in the car. The keys were in the ignition. "You guys take this and follow me. We need to get rid of the car."

Chapter Thirty-Six

The Ballroom at the Shangri-La in The Rocks, Sydney, was transformed. Fake terra cotta warriors lined the sides, forming an honour guard for the coming ceremonies. Massive Australian and Chinese flags hung on the stage, backdrops to a long table with a row of chairs on one side facing the ballroom. To the right of the table, from the point of view of the visitors and media, stood a lectern. High on the wall, on either side of the flag, were two massive screens connected to a multimedia setup.

Video playing on the screens was of mine operations in the Pilbara, the rusty red soil a backdrop to massive trucks, kilometres-long conveyors and gaping holes in the ground.

The media assembled in their designated areas, and tight security ensured that only credentialed journalists and cameramen entered the area closest to the stage.

Prime Minister Lambert and some of his senior staff were in a room off the wings. Lambert paced, fiddling with his phone. He sent a message to Vinnie. "*I need an update. Where are you?*"

He dropped into a chair, ignoring the bustle around him. Managing the schizophrenic life he'd been leading for the past few years was taking its toll. The firm but fair Prime Minister for the Australian public had to hide the black market dealings that were rapidly inflating his bank accounts. But this deal would seal it. It was the final one. He'd retire from politics in a year or so and disappear off the radar.

He took a deep breath and slowly exhaled. Stood, stretched, and smiled as President Lang Ke Shou and entourage entered the anteroom. He stuck out his hand. "President Lang. Today is the day."

Lang shook Lambert's hand and bowed. "It is indeed. Let's get this over with and celebrate. I have chartered a yacht. We'll spend the evening on the harbour celebrating the windfalls that this deal will bring."

Lambert looked around and closed his hand over his and Lang's. "Not so loud, mate."

Lang leaned into the conversation. "Windfalls for our respective countries, Prime Minister."

"Of course. I can't celebrate too much, though. I've got some proposed legislation to reverse tomorrow." He smiled and checked his watch. "We're up in a couple of minutes."

Staff took folders to the stage and placed them at the requisite places at the table. Expensive fountain pens were placed beside them.

The Prime Minister and President Lang stepped onto the stage. Lambert stepped up to the lectern, and President Lang stood to his right.

Lambert tapped on the microphone, both to confirm that it was on and to signal to the press that he was about to talk. "Good morning, everybody."

His phone vibrated. He placed it on the lectern and read the message from Vinnie. "*Be with you in a second. Big news.*" Lambert looked up at the crowd. Vinnie was someone he didn't want showing up with news of his wife in the middle of this. He couldn't see him in the room, though. He took a deep breath and continued. He smiled. "We are here today to celebrate a historic trade agreement with the Chinese government. In addition, the Chinese Government-owned company Huang Chi has agreed to acquire the Yandikoorup iron ore mine in the Pilbara. We, the Australian Government, strongly believe that trading with our largest neighbours to the north is a win-win scenario. China's investment in our small mines keeps them open, keeps the workers employed, and provides the mine with a ready market for its products. I would like to invite President Lang Ke Shou to speak a few words, and then we'll sign the contracts and answer a few of your questions." He scooped up his phone, stepped to one side and gestured for Lang to step forward.

The Chinese President adjusted the microphone slightly and spoke. "Thank you, Prime Minister. Thank you for your hospitality. We are indeed delighted to sign this agreement, which is a step forward for both of our countries. As the economy in my country grows, we need steel to build.

And the ore from the Pilbara is the highest quality ore in the world." He looked to his left at Prime Minister Lambert. "I'd like to think this is the beginning of a wonderful friendship." He swept his hand toward the table. "Shall we do the honours?"

Aides pulled the chairs out and sat the President and Prime Minister. Documents were signed, and they stood and shook hands, smiling at the flashing cameras. While holding the pose and a smile firmly fixed on his face, Lambert's phone vibrated in his pocket. He clapped the President on the back and shifted slightly behind him, pulling his phone from his pocket for a quick glance. A message from Vinnie. "*We're here.*"

Lambert slid the phone back into his pocket and stepped to the lectern, scanning the crowd. "This is the time for questions, people. What would you like to—" He stopped mid-sentence. His wife stood at the back of the room. Her two brothers stepped into the ballroom and took positions either side of her. He frowned. Stepped away from the lectern and made room for the Chinese President. He looked back at his unexpected visitors. Cheryl held up a phone and showed it to him, then typed a message. The phone in his pocket vibrated.

He placed his hand over his pocket and looked at his wife. She held up a thumb drive, smiled at him, and handed it to a tall young woman standing beside her.

Cheryl handed the thumb drive to Emma. "You can do this?"

Emma had a grin plastered across her face. "This is going to be so much fun."

Cheryl watched the young girl walk to the back of the ballroom and upstairs into a "Staff Only" door. "You trust her, Mac?"

Mac smiled. "She'll be fine."

Cameron looked up from the console used to control the audio and visual displays for the ballroom. "You're Emma?"

She held out the thumb drive. "I've got to use your machine. Which laptop controls the monitors?"

Cameron reached for the drive. "Here, I'll do it for you."

Emma yanked her hand back. "Fuck off. I'm doing this. Mac explicitly instructed me to do this. Not you." She nodded at the console with three laptops. "Which one?"

Cameron rolled his chair back and pointed at a MacBook in the middle of the equipment. "You know what to do with this?"

Emma stuck the thumb drive in the side of the laptop. "Probably. Maybe." She opened the finder and selected several files. She paused, then stepped out of the way. "Okay. You're right. I don't know this equipment." She sighed and dropped into a chair beside Cameron. "Glad you were in here. I told Mac I knew what to do, and I'd probably have fumbled my way through it eventually, but I really didn't have a clue. Would have hated to let him down."

"Fuck."

"Excuse me, Prime Minister Linda Carmody of Central Coast News Network. What was that you said?"

"Good day, Linda. Do you have a question?"

"I understand that you introduced legislation to introduce a new mining tax with the express intent to drive the mine share prices down in advance of the agreement in order to benefit the Chinese buyers. Would you care to comment?"

Other reporters sensed blood. "Sir? Would you care to comment on these allegations?"

Chapter Thirty-Seven

Lambert stammered. "Allegations of what?" He held up his hands. "Never mind that." He slid his hands in his pockets and smiled. "We believe that this agreement will pave the way to a truer free trade arrangement with one of the largest economies in the world. Imagine, if you will, building your business to serve a population of twenty-four million, and suddenly, you could serve a market *sixty times larger?*"

Carmody looked at the notepad. "Is it true that you've received gifts far above the permitted value without declaring them?"

"I'm sorry, who are you with again?"

"Central Coast News Network. Gosford. Sources have told me that you have a collection of exquisite Ming Dynasty artwork given to you by

President Lang to influence your decision regarding this trade deal, generally, and the mine purchase made by President Lang's company, specifically. Gifts worth more than ten million Australian dollars. Can you confirm that?"

"Preposterous. Somebody has been telling you falsehoods." Lambert glanced at Lang and swallowed. "These are slanderous allegations, Miss Central Coast Networks, and your station will be hearing from my legal team today." He scanned the faces of the reporters. "Any questions concerning the trade deal?" He pointed at a reporter with a hand up. "Yes, Nigel."

"Nigel Wilcox, Channel 10. This trade deal was dead in the water a couple of months ago." He looked down at his pad. Then back at the Prime Minister. "There have been reports of regular and secret meetings between you and the President at your Chief of Staff's house in Vaucluse over the past month. Can you confirm or deny that?"

Lambert rubbed the back of his neck. "Meetings between world leaders are frequently held out of the public eye. There's nothing—"

Nigel interrupted. "And where is," he checked his pad again, "Vincent Watson? He's normally by your side for events such as this. I haven't been able to reach him all day. His phone is ringing to voicemail and his assistant has been uncommunicative."

"Vinnie's running an errand for me. I'm told he should be here shortly." Lambert smiled, the questions starting to drift away from the danger area. "Vinnie's not one to pass up an open bar." He scanned the back of the ballroom. His wife was still there, not yet noticed by the press. She had a frown on her face and was looking at her watch.

"Ladies and gentlemen of the press, the focus today needs to be on the exploding Chinese market and how we can exploit that."

Nigel raised a finger. "And what's in it for China? Adding Australia to their market is a rounding error."

"Well, clearly, we are open to trade ore with China at favourable prices. But we're in Australia, Nigel. And it's 'what's in it for Australia' that you should be asking." Lambert looked at Nigel and then at Carmody. They weren't looking at him anymore.

He looked over his shoulder to see with the Chinese President was doing. Nothing.

Then he caught the images on two massive screens either side of the flags. Photos of Lambert and the Chinese President huddled together, then bank details—accounts. He recognised the details— and the amounts.

Then his wife. On screen.

The audio crackled for a second, then Cheryl's voice pierced the ballroom. He looked from the screen to the back of the room. She was live. Someone she didn't recognise was filming her with their mobile phone and projecting it through the hotel's AV system.

"Ladies and Gentlemen, I am Cheryl Watson. The Prime Minister is my husband. At least for now.

"Today, he tried to have me killed. He has been working through his CoS, Vinnie Watson, who in turn hired Dawkins and Associates to track me down and kill me. Fortunately, Dawkins hired an honest man who has been instrumental to me being able to talk to you now."

Lambert waved his arms to get the attention of the press. "This is a hoax. Disregard the ramblings of a sick woman."

Cheryl on-screen laughed. "Sick of *you*, George. Why did he want to have me killed? Funny you should ask. I have indisputable evidence of hidden bank accounts, bribes, dirty tricks, influence peddling, and tons more. I'd have passed this to authorities earlier, but Georgie has a very long reach."

Lambert pointed at Cheryl and screamed. "You're coming down with me, you fucking bitch."

The press turned as one, saw Cheryl, and converged on her, all talking at once. Lambert looked up at the screens. She was inundated with questions. He ran back to the lectern and tapped on the microphone. "Excuse me, please. Hello. The Chinese President has some words he'd like to share with you." The press stayed on Cheryl. "Hello?"

Lang walked over to him, his hands clasped in front of him. "I believe our business has concluded. You're going to be in a hell of a mess very soon. The aggravation isn't worth the small profit I'd make off

303

the mine." Lang turned, nodded at his aides, and walked off the stage.

Lambert sagged. The press had split off, and now half were yelling questions at him. Questions he had no intention of answering without his solicitor present.

Chapter Thirty-Eight

Press had died down two weeks after the big reveal. The Attorney-General's office had announced an investigation and immediately went quiet, the Prime Minister had stepped down and the Deputy PM had stepped in. A non-confidence vote triggered a new election and the ruling party was in as much disarray as any party in modern history.

Mac watched Emma working alongside Gerry in the kitchen. She was turning out to be a pretty good cook and was settling into the family like a long-lost sister.

Cheryl sat across the booth from him, leather jacket on the bench beside her, polo shirt and well-worn jeans projecting an air of wealthy-casual. She silently devoured a chicken Caesar salad.

"Ease up. It's like you haven't eaten in weeks," said Mac.

She pushed a crouton out of the bottom of the bowl and balanced it on the end of her fork. "Feels like it." She swallowed the last piece of her salad and cocked her head, looking at Mac with a critical eye. "You're a good man, Mac. Don't know how this would have ended if you hadn't been on my side." She vaguely gestured at the interior of The Pelican with her fork. "You could be doing so much better than this. Not that there's anything wrong with it here. It's nice, peaceful. Not too much press." She chuckled. "Any more."

"It's a nice place. Quiet community. I get enough business to keep my head above water. Not many people around here want to shoot me."

"I'm sure a few do." Cheryl laughed around her glass of wine. She looked past him. "So, Emma. What's her deal?"

Mac looked over his shoulder at Emma in the kitchen, washing dishes. He chuckled. "She was living on the street a couple of weeks ago. I gave up a three grand job to track her down."

Cheryl scratched her chin. "Really?" She wiped her finger along the edge of her glass was licked the taste of wine off of it. "You're too fucking nice."

"Yeah, well. It worked out for us, didn't it?"

"What was the three grand for?"

Mac took a breath and sat back in his seat. "She was klepto-ing her way through town, trying to survive. The townsfolk gathered their torches and pitchforks and demanded I find her and turn her in. Found her. Didn't seem fair to turn her in."

Cheryl shook her head. "Some tough guy you are."

Mac smiled. "Don't tell anyone. I have a rep to maintain." He leaned forward. "You're clear with all this shit? Not worried about Vinnie?"

"What, the whole taking down the government thing? Yeah. I think I'm clear." She looked around The Pelican and leaned forward. "Jane tells me that he has no memory of what put him in the hospital. Probably never will. And if he ever does, it'll be an unreliable memory. Not worried about Vinnie." She took a breath. "Dawkins' driver, though,

307

that's something else. He knows I was the one who busted his nose." She grimaced. "And he's holding out talking to the cops. For now. Thinks I'm going to give him a lot of money."

"Are you?"

"We'll see. The other side of his coin is that he was thrashed by a little woman. He'll have to live with that. We're still negotiating."

Mac chuckled. "Dawkins is pretending he has never heard of me. Pride's a nasty thing. Erased the whole week from his memory. Fortunately."

Cheryl laughed. "Short people. The Federal Police will catch up to him eventually. Can't hide from them." She pushed back her chair. "Well, I've got to run, Mac. I'd pay, but you're doing okay, right?"

"I make a buck or two."

"The money you got to find me. I know Vinnie. He would have fronted a serious amount of cash to find me." She pulled her jacket off the bench seat and shrugged it on. "Right?"

"Sure." Mac smiled wryly. "If you discount the fact that Dawkins or one of his apes broke into my place and took most of it back."

"What?"

"You're repeating yourself. What I said. I got about five grand. Not too bad."

"Bullshit. Fucking hell. What a fucking jackass that man is."

Mac took a half step back. "Jesus."

"Serious. What a twat." She took out her phone. "Give me your bank details."

"What? No."

"I'm not asking you, Mac. I'd be dead if it weren't for you." She opened her banking app and snapped her fingers. "Details."

"No. Not necessary."

"Bullshit." She put a hand on her hip. "I can find out your details if I really want you. Save me the hassle."

Mac looked at her for a second, then pulled out his phone and opened his banking app. He showed her the branch and account details. "This really isn't necessary, Cheryl. But I appreciate what you're doing."

"You have no idea, do you?"

"What? I was hired to track you down. I led the bad guys to you. Damn near got you killed." Mac shook his head. "One of the most bone-headed fucking things I've ever done." He took a deep breath and let it out slowly. "Five years as a PI, twenty-five as a cop, closest I've ever come to getting the wrong person killed."

Cheryl looked up from her phone. "Close only counts in horseshoes and hand grenades." She tapped a couple more keys on her phone. "There. You're whole again." She closed the banking app on her phone and slid it in her back pocket.

"Hang on. What does whole mean?"

"It's like the meatheads didn't break into your place."

"You can't afford that. No, no. I'm going to get the bank to reverse it."

Cheryl smiled. "George is never going to get some of his money back. I told you I wasn't lily-white in all this. I haven't killed anyone. And I haven't been treasonous. But I'll never have to work again."

She kissed him on the cheek. "Have a nice life, Mac. Don't worry about shit so much." She winked at him and walked out of the cafe.

Mac watched her leave and reopened the banking app. The balance still showed $3,437.23, but the pending balance was $203,437.23

"Fuck." He closed the app and dialled a familiar number. "Alf? The Pelican, please. I'm going to need some legal advice. Bring the best accountant you know."

He sat back in his chair and leaned back, his heart racing. Emma bounced by the table. "You okay, Mac? You look a bit off."

Mac smiled. "Just fine, Em. Grab me a pot of coffee, will you? And get some tea ready for Alf. He'll be by shortly."

"Sure thing." She sat across from him. "Listen, sorry if I was a pain before, okay? All good now?"

"Never better," said Mac. "Never better."

ABOUT THE AUTHOR

Tony McFadden is a Canadian now happily living in Australia, a land with very little snow, writing near the beach whenever possible.

You can find him on the interwebs at
www.TonyMcFadden.net,

Also by Tony McFadden

Matt's War
Daly Battles: The Fall of PyongYang
Target: Australia

G'Day LA
G'Day USA

Book 'Em
Family Matters
Unprotected Sax
(with Charles McFadden)

Have Wormhole, Will Travel
Killing Time

Mac D: Private Investigator
A Step Too Far (A Mac-D Mystery)

The Murder of Jeremy Brookes
Number Fifteen

Batteries Not Included
Broken
Dead Tomorrow
Under the Shadows

Tony McFadden